THE DEADLY FUN RUN
Abigail Summers Cozy Mysteries
Book 4

ANN PARKER

Copyright © 2024 Ann Parker

Layout design and Copyright © 2024 by Next Chapter

Published 2024 by Next Chapter

Cover art by Lordan June Pinote

This book is a work of fiction. Names, characters, places, and incidents are the product of the author's imagination or are used fictitiously. Any resemblance to actual events, locales, or persons, living or dead, is purely coincidental.

All rights reserved. No part of this book may be reproduced or transmitted in any form or by any means, electronic or mechanical, including photocopying, recording, or by any information storage and retrieval system, without the author's permission.

Also by Ann Parker

The Deadly Detective Agency
The Deadly Pub Quiz
The Deadly Regatta

*Dedicated to my beautiful daughters,
Emma Kaye & Louise Francis.*

CHARITY CAMPATHON
Fun Run & Campout

Get your tickets for a 10K run, and then camp out at Polehanger Farm on the Chiltern Hills.

Run or ramble to the top of Chittering Downs, around the beacon, and then back down to spend the night listening to bands, having a barbecue and toasting your marshmallows over the campfire.

Book your tickets now.

All proceeds go to CHAF - Children's Hospital Appeal Fund.

Get out those running trainers and dancing shoes!!!

Chapter 1

IN THE CRICKETERS INN ON BECKLESFIELD HIGH Street, the chairwoman of the Children's Hospital Appeal Fund was sitting in the corner of the bar. Penelope Aston-Whyte and the race director, Melody Myatt, were meeting with a group of sponsors for the upcoming campathon.

Drinking his single malt whisky was Harvey Bonson, owner of Bonson's Butchers, who were supplying the meat for the barbecue. Sitting next to him was the farmer, Sebastian March, who was giving up one of his larger fields for the festivities afterwards. The last to arrive was Verity Pikestaff, the glamorous co-ordinator from Gorebridge General Hospital.

Looking over her glasses at the latecomer, Penelope started the meeting by getting out a large folder and taking the lid off her gold fountain pen to take notes.

"Now we're all here, at last, let's get started. You'll be pleased to know that tickets are selling well. So far we've sold forty tickets for tents, at thirty pounds a time, and I'm pleased to say that one hundred and fifty people have signed up for the fun run at twenty pounds each."

"And we've still got three weeks to go yet," said Melody.

"How many tents have you got room for at Polehanger Farm, Sebastian?"

The smart-looking farmer rubbed his chin. "Fifty maximum, I reckon. I'll have to get extra portaloos ordered now."

The Bonson Butchers' owner sat forward. "Now look here, when I said I'd provide the meat for the barbecues and sausages for breakfast, you said nowt about that many going. I'll be bankrupt if you don't watch out," he said in a strong northern accent.

"Hardly," said Penelope. "You own the largest chain of butchers in the south. I'm sure you'll be fine. And don't forget all the publicity you'll get. I heard the local television channel is covering it, and it's been in the papers. After all, we have got a world-famous band headlining. And they're doing it for free."

Sebastian asked, "I don't want any promotion like Harvey. All I want to know is who this famous band is. Can't you even tell us, Penelope?"

"No. That was part of the agreement. I can quite understand it. If everyone knows who they are and it gets out, all the fans will turn up and there wouldn't be room for the runners. There would be havoc on the night."

"Good, keep it quiet. You'll get no more meat off me than what we agreed. No more than fifty tents then," said Harvey. "And I want plenty of signs with the Bonson's logo on, pet."

"I'm definitely not your pet. But thank you, Harvey. You and Sebastian have already been mentioned in the press and it will say Bonsons on all the flags. Now Melody is going to give us an update on what she's been doing."

Melody opened her notebook and said, "I've tried to get as many donations for things as I can, so we owe a huge thank you to Chiltern Springs, who have agreed to supply the water for the drinking stations all the way up and down Chittering Downs. To keep in line with our green theme, they're giving out drinks in paper cups rather than bottles. Er, I've found someone who will make and put up the flags. And someone to supply the marshmallows and sticks for free, so we can sell them for profit. We're going to hire a couple of fire pits to toast them on. But that is very reasonable. Chilly Ices is having an ice cream van near the start, and I've been in touch with the council and they've agreed to shut the lanes and put up diversion signs from midnight to midnight. The only thing we are a bit short on, is volunteer marshals for the day. People would rather give up money than time."

Verity Pikestaff spoke for the first time. "I might be able to help with that. There's a lot of staff and patients at the hospital that would love to run, but they aren't fit enough, so I'm sure they will want to do their bit."

"That's good. Thank you. Have you put the posters up yet at the hospital?"

"Yes, and I've put out flyers. The advert is coming out in the next edition of the Chiltern Weekly."

"Good," said Penelope. "Because we need plenty of spectators to put money in the buckets that people will be walking around with. There are two companies that I need to get in touch with that have promised help or a large donation for their names as sponsors. Let me see, er, I had phone calls from Walker & Francis Pharmaceuticals, a drug company, if any of you have heard of them, and Estryke Bikes. And The Marquee Company has promised us a large one for free. We need all the help we can get so that the kids get as much as possible. Is there any other business or shall we have another drink first? Mine's a white wine."

After another round was bought by the young farmer, they got down to talking about times and the amount of rolls and salad that they might need. This would have to come out of their own funds unless they found a donor.

"Don't expect me to cough up," said Harvey. "I've done my bit."

"We didn't think you would. I'm not too sure why you even

got involved in the first place. You seem to be doing everything possible to spend as little as you can," said Penelope.

"It was the wife's idea. The hospital took care of our bonny granddaughter a few years back, so I said I'd help out. Didn't realise you'd have the shirt off my back though."

Sebastian rolled his eyes. "Put the bread rolls on my bill, Penelope."

"Aye, when you think about it, all you're giving is an empty field," added the butcher.

"And the toilets, and the stage, and sorting out the parking. I'm seriously wondering why nobody has ever smacked you one."

"Plenty have tried, believe me. But you're welcome to come outside and try yourself, laddie."

"Please boys, that's enough," said Penelope. "We're very grateful to both of you. Now, Harvey, don't forget that you have to supply a vegetarian option as well."

The butcher turned red. "What? I'm a butcher. The world's gone mad. My dad would turn in his grave."

"The world has simply moved on from killing animals, Harvey. I'm a vegan myself," said Melody.

"Don't even get me started on vegans, lassie! I can see I'm outnumbered, so okay, I'll get the wife to supply some. It was her idea to volunteer, so she should do something. I don't want anything to do with that kind of blasphemy. Vegetarians, huh. I've been eating meat all my life and it's done me no harm."

Penelope raised her eyebrows at the overweight butcher, who looked like he had high blood pressure, but just said, "Perhaps now is the time to close the meeting and call it a day. So, Sebastian, if you could sort out those things for us, that would be marvellous. I know you'll do what's needed. Now before I forget, Verity, can you give me the financial printouts for the donations we've raised for you in the past? Oh, and what you've spent the money on."

"Whatever for? I've never been asked that by anyone else. They leave it up to us where we spend the money. I can assure you that it all goes to the children or the ward. Last time, if I remember rightly, we bought extra folding beds so the parents could stay and toys and books for the playroom. Plus equipment that the nurses requested. I expect I've got the receipts somewhere."

"Well then, you've got nothing to worry about, have you?" Penelope closed her folder and said, "I don't know about you, but I could do with another drink."

Within two hours, one of the five people in that bar would be dead.

In Gorebridge, Lydia Aston-Whyte was looking out of the office window. The boss had gone and she decided she would go herself. So what if she got the boot. She had been working at Sutton Insurance for six months now. One more week and she might die of boredom, if that was possible. Lydia was beginning to regret leaving home and moving into the shared flat. Although she had her freedom, she couldn't do much because she had to pay the rent. She'd been so excited to move out, envisaging parties and friends staying over, but the only thing she gained was the responsibility of paying bills and tidying up after herself. Her flatmates were worse than her mum if she left her plate unwashed on the side. At least at her mum's house she didn't have to pay for anything or do any housework. But she was twenty-one now; she should be out on her own.

But it wasn't that great. She was on her own but was missing her home comforts: a nice garden, cable TV, and all the food she could eat. There, she had a view of the Downs; at her flat, she had a view of the paper factory. And she had to admit, although her mum could be a control freak, she was actually missing her and their chats. So she decided to drive to Becklesfield and see her mother.

Lydia checked that no one was looking and got her bag and phone out of the drawer, then she sneaked out. The other two girls didn't even notice. At least she had a nice car, she thought, as she started the engine. Her mother had bought it for her twenty-first birthday, bless her. She wasn't that bad. Lydia was getting close to home when her phone pinged, as a text came through. She pulled over in case it was work, but she smiled to herself; it was her mum, who texted that the meeting at the Cricketers had gone well and asked if she had booked her place on the 10K run. Also, could she pop to Becklesfield and help her with the leaflets as soon as she could.

She took back all the nice things that she had just been thinking about her mother. She was still trying to run her life. She texted back that she had a day off and would be there soon. More to have something to eat than help with the fun run. Then another text came through, telling her that the silly cat had got stuck on the roof again, and she was going to get the ladder out and would see her later. That was the last text that she would ever receive from her mother, Penelope Aston-Whyte.

Chapter 2

POLICE CONSTABLES TOM BENNETT AND JANE NICHOLS got the message not long before they were going to finish for the day. An elderly man had heard a noise and found his neighbour lying under a ladder in her front garden. They needed to attend and treat it as a crime scene, but more than likely it was an accident. The paramedics had pronounced her dead, and the lady's daughter, Lydia Aston-Whyte, had arrived and would meet them there. The address was High Tops, Bellringer Close, Becklesfield.

They stopped the police car outside the row of five large bungalows made of flint, as an agitated young lady with an unlikely shade of blonde hair ran out to meet them.

"Please help. Something awful has happened. My mother's dead. I got here just after Dr Boyes had found Mum. I can't believe it."

Jane said, "We're so sorry for your loss, Miss Aston-Whyte. She fell from a ladder, is that right?"

"Lydia, please. Not fell from it. It looks like it went sideways. She's round here."

Penelope was lying on her back and the top rung of the ladder was over her legs. Her glasses were on the ground two feet away and looked in better shape than their owner. Tom thought she looked about fifty, which made him think of his own mother. The auburn-haired lady was wearing a mustard-coloured jacket and green, tartan trousers. Her eyes were open and her whole face had a look of fear. He could only imagine those few seconds as the ladder toppled over sideways.

"Why would your mother have been up the ladder?" asked Tom.

"Roary. I swear she loved that cat more than she loved me." She pointed to a grey tabby sitting on the doorstep as if he hadn't got a care in the world, let alone caused someone's death. "She texted me to say that he was stuck on the roof again and she was going to get him down."

"Did this happen often?" asked Jane.

"Put it this way, he was on the roof so much, people called him Fiddler. I suppose Mum went up the ladder and lost her balance. Perhaps I should mention that she had spent the last couple of hours in the Cricketers. They had a meeting of the fun run committee."

"Me and one of my colleagues are running in that," said Tom. "And my wife," he added with a frown.

"I was supposed to. I can't even think of that now."

"Do you live here, Miss?"

"Not at the moment. I've got my own flat. I'd left work early, so when Mum texted me to help with some leaflets, I came over. If only I'd left five minutes earlier."

The two paramedics asked if they could take Penelope away, but Tom took a few photos of the body just in case.

"What happens now? Can I go and make some phone calls? I've got to let my brother and Dad know." Lydia suddenly realised what had happened and burst into tears as her mother's body was taken on the trolley to the ambulance. "I'm sorry."

Jane put an arm around her and helped her into the house. "Is there anyone I can call for you, Lydia?"

"I'm ringing Dad. They're divorced, but he should know. He'll want to see me, and I want him to come."

Jane left her to phone her family and was surprised to see Tom putting up crime scene tape. "Let's take a few more photos just in case, but it looks like an accident, doesn't it, Jane? Poor lady. I'll phone it in."

At least there was a body that Hayley and the other detectives didn't have to be told about this time. This was no murder; simply a tragic accident.

Chapter 3

THE BECKLESFIELD PUBLIC LIBRARY HAD CLOSED FOR the day, so the resident ghosts and members of The Deadly Detective Agency were discussing who was their favourite television detective.

"No doubt about it," said Betty. "Jessica Fletcher. I loved that show. Especially all the ones in Cabot Cove with Doc Hazlitt. There were as many murders there as in Becklesfield."

"No way was she the best," said Lillian. "She solved most murders by confronting them, then they said, 'Yes, I dunnit,' and the sheriff just happened to be there. I just wonder why no one ever said it was them, and then shot her. But that would have spoiled the series I guess. I liked Columbo myself."

"Jessica Fletcher wasn't on when I was alive, so my favourite is the Basil Rathbone films, when he was Sherlock Holmes. They were good. Now he was a brilliant sleuth."

"That's showing your age, Terry. It was an actor called Jeremy Brett in my day. I can't decide whether mine is Hercule Poirot or Miss Marple. Both amazing, and kept you guessing till the end," said Abigail. She had been a dressmaker in life, and the pretty thirty-nine-year-old had started the agency when they had all solved her murder before the police did.

"Like you do," said Suzie. "I can see you in a TV show - *The Abigail Summers Murder Mysteries.*" Suzie was a beautiful, black girl, who had been run over and killed by a drunk driver.

"Hmm, *The Abigail Summers Murder Mysteries.* I like that idea. They could have a beautiful, young, sexy actress play me."

"Oh, I thought it would be based on you," said Terry as he smiled at the others.

"And an old codger to play Terry Styles," joked Abigail. She and Terry had been on quite a few dates, where usually a murder or something happened, but they were very fond of each other, and the *love* word had even been mentioned on occasion.

"We haven't had a murder for a few weeks, have we?" said Suzie.

"Well, I'm sure we don't want anyone to die for us, sweetheart." Lillian Yin had looked after Suzie after she had died. She was still in her nurse's uniform and had met the nine-year-old when she had been knocked down, and had been there for her ever since.

"No?" said Abigail. "No, of course we don't. It's a shame though. We haven't had a case since Arnold Trippet delivered more than just logs to Mrs Mud. Not realising Mr Mud had fitted a camera in their bedroom."

"Even Johnson couldn't get that wrong," said Terry.

"Although he nearly did. He really thought that Mr Mud had accidentally choked to death on eating popcorn in bed. Good job that we saw the camera lens in between the books on the shelf, that showed the two lovers stuffing it in his mouth."

Betty held up a finger. "Don't forget Sconegate. That was very nasty."

Abigail said, "Yes, but I'm not sure that Hayley stopping a bun fight at the Women's Institute garden party counts as a case."

"Mrs Scrimshaw cheated in the scone competition. That's akin to treason, and that still carries the death penalty."

"I'll take your word for it, Betty. I was never asked to join. I expect it was because I was too young."

"More like too bossy," whispered Lillian to Suzie.

Abigail gave her one of her 'if looks could kill if you weren't already dead' looks. "I heard that, you two."

Betty said, "I think we should be very grateful for Abigail turning us into sleuths ourselves. I know I thank you from the heart of my bottom." Betty had a vast knowledge of sayings, but very rarely got them in the right order. But that was part of her charm.

"Aw, and I thank you from mine as well. But you know me, I don't like to brag. What? When have you ever heard me brag?"

They all started talking at once, each remembering the separate times.

"Maybe once or twice then," admitted Abigail. "But seriously, we need to get some of the Deads to contact us like before. Perhaps you could do some more adverts for the agency, Suzie."

"Of course. I'll get Hayley to get the paper and pens again."

"And maybe Hayley's advert for our services on her website will get us some small jobs. It doesn't have to be murder, I suppose. Although, I can't remember one of Miss Marple's thirteen problems being about a missing cat or a lost ring. Why don't we have a look around the village. There might be something going on. Maybe we could pop in and see Hayley."

Betty said, "Unless she's out training for her marathon again. It's funny, she never came across as sporty before."

Abigail added, "I know. She doesn't like walking much, let alone running. I can remember when she took the car to go to church once."

"Ah, but in her defence it was raining," said Terry. "We'll have to go and watch on the day. I heard Lady Caroline is doing it with her. The 10K is for charity for the children's ward. That's where you worked, wasn't it, Lillian?"

"It was. I'd have loved to do it for them, if I wasn't dead. It's not fair."

"You still could, Lillian. We'll cheer you on. I suppose we all could run. What is 10K anyway? We didn't have Ks in my day, only miles. What is happening to the world? They'll be getting rid of inches soon," said Terry.

"What are inches?" joked Suzie. "It's centimetres and metres now."

"Progress, I'm afraid, Terry. I think it's about five or six miles. So who is up for a walk round the village, not a run?" said Abigail.

"I'll come. If I don't, you're sure to come across a dead body or something," said Betty, who, at eighty-two years old, loved all the sleuthing. She had been married to John for sixty years and had died a week after he did. So now she called this her *me-time*. Lillian said she would wait in the library, and Suzie said she would stay too and read her two new magazines that had come in that day. Only she could turn the pages or move objects.

It was a warm autumn evening, and the village had quietened down for the day as Terry, Abigail, and Betty strolled down the high street. All the shops had closed their doors, and Mrs Merry was locking up the florist's. The few people that were about were going into the Cricketers Inn. As they neared the village green, Terry pointed to a lady walking up and down by the church wall and looking very flustered. He knew she was a newly Dead straight away. He had been greeting them for the last fifty years and was always there to explain what had happened to them. He thought the latest arrival looked about his age, fiftyish, with auburn hair, and wearing a mustard-coloured jacket and green tartan trousers.

Chapter 4

TOM BENNETT WAS LATE HOME AFTER THE ACCIDENT report for Penelope Aston-Whyte had been written up. His wife, Hayley, opened a bottle of beer for him, and he flopped on the sofa.

"Anything happen at work today, hun?"

Tom shook his head. "Nothing much. A team of shoplifters in town, and just before we finished, Jane and I had a call-out to Becklesfield, Bellringers Close. Poor old lady fell off a ladder," and he gave her a quick recap.

"What was she doing up a ladder?"

Tom looked at the ball of fur that was purring loudly on his lap. Luna, the kitten that they had saved from near-death, never left him alone once he got home. "To rescue her cat, Roary. He has a habit of getting stuck on the roof apparently. He must have got down himself, though, because he was on the porch."

"So the cat had nine lives, but not her then. Poor thing."

"Yes, it was sad. She was about my mum's age."

"No, I mean the poor cat. What will happen to little Roary?"

"No, you can't have him! Anyway, she had a daughter, Lydia Aston-Whyte. She was very upset, of course."

The Deadly Fun Run

"It wasn't Penelope who died, was it?" said Hayley in shock.

"Yes, it was. Do you know her?"

"She's the main organiser for the campathon. I wonder if it will still go ahead."

"The daughter seemed to think it would. No doubt there'll be someone else to take over, I expect. They can't really cancel it. There're only a few weeks left. I still can't believe you're doing the 10K. We've been married for four years, and I don't think I've ever seen you run."

"Rubbish, I ran to the shop the other day."

"It must have been about to shut, then."

"That's beside the point. We needed milk."

Tom started to laugh. "Hey, maybe you shouldn't. I've just remembered how much you like to win. Your mum always mentions what you were like as a kid. You know, when all hell would break loose if you didn't win pass the parcel. Even when it wasn't your birthday."

"You should have seen me playing musical chairs," she said guiltily. "But I'm not like that now, hun."

"What about the pub quiz, then?"

"I would have won that easily if someone hadn't died and spoiled it. Anyway, Caroline said she's going to get me into her gym, and we can do some proper training. I might stand a chance of beating the others then."

Lady Caroline Hatton of Chiltern Hall was Hayley's good friend. She often helped with their cases. Hayley was a psychic medium, who used the name Hayley Moon when working. Her life had changed when her deceased dressmaker, Abigail Summers, had burst into her house, telling her she had been murdered and needed Hayley's help to solve it. Of course, it helped having Tom on their side, but that wasn't always willingly. So life had never been the same, or as exciting, since then.

"Which gym is it? The one in town?"

"As if. No, we're going to the Courtridge Hotel and Spa, hun."

"Lucky you. Very nice. I've driven past. It's the one that looks like a castle."

"I know. Actually, it was a castle many years ago. Some millionaire snapped up the derelict ruins and did it up. It will probably take him about twenty years to start getting his money back," said Hayley.

"Her money. It's an American lady, I heard somewhere. Well, I'll be training in Gyms 4 U in Gorebridge. Then we might just go jogging." Tom and his friend, Sergeant Dave Mills, were running on behalf of the police station in Gorebridge.

"Are Dave and Isabella camping afterwards? We could make a night of it."

"I'll ask. But that's a good idea. If they aren't, we still could. I haven't camped since I was a kid. I think Mum and Dad have still got the tent, save buying one."

"Tents have changed a bit, though, hun. You can get ones that go up in minutes now. And I bet it's like the one we had, with a hundred poles and heavy canvas. I'll have a look online."

"Yeah, it must be over twenty years old. But don't go spending too much. I know you; you like your bed and home comforts. We'll probably only use it once."

"I won't. But they supply the food, so all we need to take is some drink, blow-up beds, and sleeping bags. I'll get the tickets. I daresay someone else will take on Penelope's job. Perhaps she was rushing with all she had to do and fell."

"More than likely. Anyway, Hayl, you needn't get involved this time, thank goodness. I had a word with the neighbour who found her, and he didn't see anything suspicious. They'll have to do an autopsy, but it looks like an accidental death." But then Tom shuddered as a swirl of deathly cold air filled the room.

"Accidental death, my Aunt Sally! Penelope Aston-Whyte

was murdered!" Abigail shouted. Tom looked around and knew immediately who had arrived, even though he couldn't hear or see them. They were back. He turned on the TV and turned the volume up loud.

Hayley whispered, "Let's go in the conservatory where Tom can't hear us, or rather hear me. Well, welcome to my house, Penelope. I was so sorry to hear about your accident."

"That's what I've been telling these people. I went up the ladder and then heard the gravel crunch as if someone was walking on it. But before I could see who it was, the ladder was pushed over. By some force, I might add. Then I heard footsteps running away."

"How awful for you. I'm so sorry. My husband, Tom, was one of the officers called to the scene, and they thought it looked like an accident, so I'm not sure what I can do. They're doing a post-mortem, probably in the next few days, but if they can't see any evidence of foul play that will be that. Unless you know who did it, I don't know how we can change their minds. If you've been ill and the pathologist finds something, then it will make them even more sure."

"How about three large glasses of white wine?" said Penelope with a sigh.

"That would do it as well. Tom said something about a cat."

"Yes, Roary was on the roof again. But I've never had a problem getting him down before. I think he liked the attention."

"You're probably right. Tom said he was sitting on the porch without a care in the world."

"Charming. But that sounds about right."

"My husband also said your daughter was there and she was very upset. Lydia, isn't it? So, had you been to the pub?"

"Yes, the Cricketers. I don't know if you've heard about the campathon, but we had a meeting there."

"I have. I'm actually running with Lady Caroline Hatton. And we were just talking about doing the camping as well. I hope it still goes ahead."

"I'm sure it will. Melody Myatt knows everything that I know. And I keep a folder with all my notes and contacts in. I can't understand who would do it. The meeting went off fine. There was a bit of a tiff between the men, but that was the only thing out of the ordinary. So, I can't believe it had anything to do with someone wanting to kill me. Bonson, yes."

"The butcher?" said Abigail.

"Yes, Harvey Bonson. He was there as the main donor for the barbecue and breakfast. He fell out with Sebastian March. He's the farmer whose land we're holding it on. Harvey thought he was giving more than the empty field, like he was. He's not known for his generosity. But Sebastian was doing a lot more than that. They nearly had a punch-up about it, but it blew over."

"Who else was there?"

"Melody Myatt, the race director. She's my right hand, so I can't think it would have been her. That only leaves Verity Pikestaff, the coordinator for the hospital. We all had a few drinks and left amicably. I walked home, of course. I wouldn't have driven. But I was perfectly capable of going up a ladder. Who knew that cat would be the death of me."

"You can't blame the cat, hun. I've been worrying about him. Will he be alright?"

"When I've been away before, Dr Boyes, my neighbour, has fed him. And maybe Lydia will look after him. Poor Lydia. Can you help me, please, Hayley? I know how good you are. I was at the Women's Institute meeting when you gave a talk, so I know what you're capable of."

"I can't make the CID start a murder inquiry, Penelope. Have you ever heard of DCI Johnson? No? Then you're lucky. He hates me, and he hates Tom. Mainly because we've solved cases before he does. So, he's not going to listen to me. I think what I could do is talk to your daughter and see if she can suggest that it might be murder. Have you got any enemies at all?"

"Or you could have seen something that you shouldn't have," said Abigail.

"If I did, I missed it. I've got an ex - Malcolm. But we're happily divorced. Although, I did get the house, and he wasn't too pleased about that. But that was years ago. He moved on and got married, so he's settled again now. Lydia was hard work as a teenager, but she's got her own place, and she wouldn't push me off a ladder. My son, Calum, and my daughter-in-law live in Suffolk. I can't say Vanessa and I get on, but she wouldn't want me dead. Well, she might, but I can't see her doing it."

Terry asked if the neighbour who said he found her could have had a motive.

"Not Dr Boyes. But his wife and I had a very volatile relationship. It started three years ago when she refused to chop down a tree that was stopping my light, so I had it cut right down from my side. Then I noticed all my roses were dying that were on her side of the garden. I knew she'd been spraying them with weed killer. So, I accidentally cut all the flowers off her hydrangeas that were blooming in her front garden."

"So maybe she accidentally pushed the ladder over," said Abigail.

"Murder is a bit different to a few pranks."

"People love their gardens and have murdered for less, haven't they?"

"I think I remember Dr Boyes from my appointments at the hospital," said Betty. "A nice man as I remember."

"He's retired now. I'm glad he found me and not her. She would have been as happy as Larry. Wonder she didn't. She's the nosiest person I've ever met."

"Tom had a word with him, and he said he didn't see anyone else there."

"Well, he would do if his wife had sent her flying," said Abigail bluntly. "We need to go and see if there are any footprints. It was gravel, but there might be some somewhere. And we'll check on the cat, Penelope."

"Thank you. I think I'll go with you and see how Lydia is."

Hayley frowned. "I'm wondering if I should go to see her now as well. But do I say that you've contacted me? People are very suspicious if I turn up. They automatically think I'm after money."

"She's not shown any interest in the supernatural that I know. I'm not sure that she would believe you."

"If you're there, I'm sure we can make her believe. I've been tested before. It's just that I don't want to scare her if she's on her own, hun."

"I see what you mean, Hayley. But she's a strong, young woman, and she could always go and stay with her dad. If we hurry, she should still be there. She moved out a while ago and got a job and a flat in Gorebridge, so let's go now while she's still at my house. Well, it used to be my house," said Penelope sadly.

Abigail squeezed her hand. "I know what you're going through. I was murdered as well and lost my lovely cottage. But don't worry, we aren't going to stop until we've caught the ba… the person that did this. So, Betty and I will drop in on the Boyes, and Terry, Hayley, and you can go and see Lydia and make sure that she is okay."

And poor Tom had to cook his own dinner, again.

Mrs Boyes looked out of her bay window and said to her husband, who was drinking a cup of tea and reading his paper, "What is she doing here?"

Dr Boyes didn't answer. His wife spent half her life looking through the net curtain at the front of the house, wondering what people were doing.

"Arthur! Arthur! Listen to me when I'm shouting at you. It's that Hayley Moon, the psychic woman. Well, Hayley Bennett to be exact. What's she doing here?" Ingrid Boyes repeated.

"Contacting the dead, obviously," he answered sarcastically.

"I bet Lydia got hold of her to see if Penelope's still here. Probably wants to know her mum's PIN number for her bank account."

"Why do you always have to see the worst in people? She's just lost her mother, so leave it alone for once."

"She's ringing the doorbell now. Lydia's letting her in. What did I tell you? Perhaps I'll go round tomorrow to give her a sympathy card and find out."

"Lydia won't tell you a thing. She knows what you thought of her mum, so don't be such a hypocrite. Ingrid, I mean it, get away from that window, now!"

"Don't be silly, dear. This is the most exciting thing that's ever happened in the Close. And I'm right in the middle of it," she said excitedly. "I can't wait to ring Shirley and tell her all the gossip. I'm just annoyed that you found her and I didn't. I blame you. If I hadn't been starting your tea, it would have been me. I wouldn't be surprised if it was a murder, Arthur. If I had been standing here, I might have even seen who did it. I can't have been the only one that wished she would die."

Arthur Boyes looked at his wife and wondered if she had been anywhere near that ladder. She could have done it, and then ran around to the side gate and in the back door, so he realised that he couldn't rule it out for sure. He rubbed his arms as he felt that a sudden chill had filled the room. Betty and Abigail had heard his wife's words and were wondering the same thing.

"And you think I'm nosy," said Abigail. "Poor old thing, she missed a murder, literally right on her own doorstep."

Betty said, "That's karma for you. Mind you, I was a bit of a curtain-twitcher myself. If I stood in the right place upstairs in my bedroom, I could see the entire cul-de-sac."

Abigail smiled, "Me too, Betty. I could see even more if I stood on the chair. That's probably why we're so good at sleuthing, in our defence. I always did like to know what's going on."

"I'd say we were more caring about others, dear."

"Absolutely. Someone once said it would be the death of me. And in a way, it was. But maybe we shouldn't mention this to the others. And you know what curiosity did to the cat, don't you, Betty? Do you?"

"I know a cat can look at a queen, but I've a feeling curiosity got it killed. Which is ironic as the cat next door got its owner killed. It's probably why we always had dogs."

"This Boyes woman doesn't seem to have a nice thing to say about anyone."

"I feel sorry for her husband. I bet he wishes he hadn't retired."

"Long-suffering is the word, Betty. It might have given him an idea of what to do if she ever goes up a ladder herself. It doesn't sound like she's going to miss her neighbour."

"I think she will. She obviously got a lot of pleasure out of hating her. I wonder if she hated her enough to kill her."

Next door, Lydia had invited Hayley in, but then she began to regret it when she said why she was there: that her mother had visited her. A likely story. If she was after money she wouldn't be getting any. She hadn't got any till she could see what her mum had lying about. And what with the police and now this weirdo, she hadn't had the chance to look.

"So what did she say?" Lydia asked sarcastically.

"She said, have you booked your place in the fun run yet?"

"Mum asked me that on the text before she died. You could have seen that somehow. Get out before I call the police."

"Mum says you always were a sceptic. You only believed in the tooth fairy for the cash. But when you saw the film *Poltergeist*, when you were ten, you couldn't sleep for a week."

Lydia felt goosebumps. "Lots of kids get scared after seeing that. Ask her what the name of our last cat was."

"Oscar."

"My best friend at primary school?"

"Donna."

"Um, who was my first boyfriend?"

"Billy. She said we were hoping you were going to stay with him."

"Our last dog?"

"She says, nice try, Lydsy Lou, we never had a dog. She prefers cats."

Lydia was frowning and couldn't think straight. This couldn't be happening. She started to breathe heavily, and Hayley told her to sit back and relax.

"Slow breaths, hun, and then blow out. We know this is a shock for you, but Penelope needs your help, but more than that, she needs you to know that she is all right. She knows you're strong enough to handle this."

"I'm not strong. I couldn't even make it in that flat. I miss her so much already. Please tell her." Tears had formed in her eyes.

"She can hear you, and she's not going anywhere. She says, can you look after Roary? It's going to be okay. There's some money in an envelope behind the mirror in her bedroom. Enough to keep you going till the executor of the will gets in touch. She's organised everything for you. The will is in her walnut bureau in the dining room."

"Ask her what the hell was she doing up that ladder? The cat always got down in the end. Why lose your life for him and leave me all on my own?"

Hayley knelt in front of Lydia and held her hands. "Lydia,

this is going to be hard to hear, and I'm so sorry to have to tell you this, but I need you to be strong. Mum came to me because she didn't fall; she was pushed."

"Murdered? You mean someone did it on purpose?"

"That's what she says, and I believe her. But the police are convinced that it's an accident, so we need you to get in touch with Sergeant Dave Mills at Gorebridge Police Station. Say what we've told you, but you can't mention me. That wouldn't help at all, I'm afraid. The boss of CID, Detective Chief Inspector Johnson, hates me, so don't speak to him, just Mills."

"But who did it? Does she know?"

"No, unfortunately she heard footsteps and then felt the big push. And then she heard someone running away. But don't worry, she didn't suffer. She thinks she must have hit her head on the concrete path. She loves you so much and hates to see you suffering. She didn't get on that well with your dad, but he's a good man and he will look after you."

"Daddy's on his way. He should be here soon, Mummy," she said and started to sob.

Hayley sat next to her and put an arm around her shoulder, while Penelope could only look on. But Terry put his arm around her and gave it a squeeze.

"Can you think of anyone who would have wanted your mother dead, Lydia?"

"She could be annoying, sorry Mum. But no, I can't think of anyone. She loved helping people. Look at all she does for CHAF. And, Mum, I will do the run in your honour."

"Your mum's saying all the details are in the folder on the hall table, if you can get it, please. Which she says you'll need to give to Melody Myatt. She's the race director, and should be able to carry on with all the preparations."

"I know Melody. Will do. Here you are, Hayley. You go through it. I don't think I can." The thick ringed folder was a testament to how hard Penelope had worked to get the fun run, well, up and running, thought Hayley.

"You're very organised, Penelope. Here we are – Meeting at Cricketers. Present: Penelope Ashton-Whyte of CHAF. Melody Myatt, Race Organiser and Race Director. Verity Pikestaff, Hospital Coordinator. Sebastian March, donor. Harvey Bonson, donor."

Penelope added, "That was all of us. We had a drink and I made sure everything was getting done."

"What are they like? Could it be one of them?"

"Melody is nice. I can't think it would be her. Bonson had double whiskies and was getting tiresome. Challenged March to go outside and it nearly got physical. I asked Verity for the paperwork for the other times we collected for the children's ward at Gorebridge, and thinking about it, she got very defensive. Accused me of not trusting her." Hayley retold everything to Lydia.

"So maybe she had something to hide." Hayley read all the notes. She had always been a fast reader. "We'll need to tell the police to question them all. It could easily be one of them. Don't worry, Lydia, I'll be with you all the way. Will you stay here and look after Roary? Your mum will be very grateful."

Lydia smiled for the first time. "I suppose I could give up my small, overcrowded bedsit in the middle of Gorebridge, for this detached, spacious house with a lovely garden. If she really wants me to. For the sake of Roary, of course."

"That's my girl," said Penelope.

"I'm going to get off," said Hayley. "Good luck with the police. I'll leave you my number. It's not going to be easy. You'll have to say that you have a feeling or something. Or say that your mum could get up and down a ladder like a rat."

"Don't worry, I'll think of something. Ask Mum, I was good at making up stories when I wanted to get my own way."

"That's true," said Penelope.

"I can't face doing it today, though. It will have to be tomorrow. Dad can take me. Is Mum going to stay here for a while? I don't mind as long as she doesn't scare me."

"Of course she is, hun. She just wants to make sure that you're alright till your father gets here. Take my card and let me know how you get on, please. And don't forget to ask for Sergeant Dave Mills."

Hayley and Terry left Penelope with Lydia and couldn't help but think that her mother had made things a lot worse for the grieving daughter. Hayley had a sudden feeling of being watched and turned to see the neighbour, Mrs Boyes, jump back from the window. She might be worth speaking to. If not a suspect, Hayley imagined that not much went on in Bellringer Close that she didn't know about.

"She doesn't know anything," shouted Abigail as she came out of the house with Betty. "Believe me, she would be the first to say. She hasn't stopped talking about it. That poor husband needs earplugs, I should think. We had a look, and even with her bay window, anyone coming from the right of where the ladder was would have been hidden. I feel a bit sorry for her. She's spent her entire life waiting for the biggest gossip, and when it happens, she misses it. Although, she did say that it could have been murder, mainly because she had wished her dead herself. So she is potentially a suspect, I suppose."

Betty added, "And she didn't even get to find the body. Her husband heard a crash and went out to look before she could, and she missed the pleasure of that as well. Serves her right, I reckon. I can't abide anyone that spies on their neighbours," she said, winking at Abigail. "She was dying to know what the medium, Hayley Moon, was doing next door. Honestly, she doesn't miss a thing."

"Poor woman," said Hayley. "I actually feel sorry for her. If there was something nice in her life, she wouldn't feel the need to look at others."

"You're so tolerant, Hayley. I just think she's a nosy old bag," said Abigail. "Could Lydia help us?"

"Yes, she was a star. She's going to think of something to say to the police so they look at it in more detail. I don't have a lot of confidence in her succeeding, though. I know from Tom, the police have enough to do without investigating accidents."

"And if Johnson gets to hear of it, we might as well just forget it."

Chapter 5

THE FOLLOWING MORNING, HAYLEY WAS REALLY looking forward to meeting Lady Caroline at the Courtridge Hotel and Spa. Unfortunately, it wasn't for coffee and cake but their first workout session. Caroline had booked a personal trainer, who Hayley had assumed would be a lady, but it turned out to be a blond, good-looking man from Sweden. She began to wish that she had exercise gear like the rest of the members were wearing, rather than a round-neck T-shirt and leggings. All the other ladies sported bright-coloured lycra and pristine designer trainers.

Erik started them off with light stretches, which Hayley thought wasn't bad at all. But by the end of the hour, she realised how out of shape she was. Caroline suggested they should then go on the treadmills for a while, but Hayley managed to get her to agree to a swim in the pool instead. Caroline wanted to have a walk round the grounds before they went, and Hayley agreed, even though her body and legs ached. But she thought it would give them a chance to talk about the case, as Caroline knew all the major players in the different charities in the county. Hayley was glad she had put her coat on, as the weather was definitely getting cooler and the leaves were turning brown.

"I've actually been roped in to help on the fun run committee and start the race. I think all the local celebrities expected expenses. Melody Myatt phoned last night. She's taking over from Penelope. So I'm meeting with the others at the Cricketers this afternoon."

"Rather you than me. I don't think I'd have the energy. I'll probably be bedridden by five o'clock. Promise me you'll tell me all the details, won't you?"

"Of course. I'll try and ask some questions about her death."

"Well, be careful. One of them could be a murderer."

There was a bench halfway round, and Hayley told Caroline that she should get going as she needed to stop for a while. In actual fact, every muscle ached, and she was beginning to think that Tom was right; she'd be lucky to get to the bottom of Chittering Downs, let alone up and down again. She closed her eyes and felt a presence next to her. Hayley opened one eye and could make out a young man on her left. He had large, innocent eyes and a long fringe of dark, wavy hair.

"Wow, you can see me."

Hayley was so tempted to pretend she couldn't. It wouldn't be the first time, and she was absolutely shattered. "No, I can't hear a thing."

"So you can. Marvellous."

"Yes, I can see you. As long as you don't want me to move. I don't think I can, hun. If it's to pass on a message, I could do that tomorrow, if I'm still alive."

"A teeny weeny bit more than that. I need you to dig up my bones."

"You what?!" said Hayley, opening her eyes and taking a good look at him for the first time.

"You don't have to do it now. Tomorrow will do."

"You'd better tell me your name first. I'm Hayley."

"I wish I could. I can't even say for sure how long I've been dead. Seems like years. It was before this hotel was built. I remember everything since I died, but nothing before. I think there have been about twelve winters. I've no idea how old I am either."

"You look about eighteen to me." Hayley felt so sorry for the young boy, who was dressed in jeans and a black hoodie, which had an eagle emblem on the front. His clothes were covered in soil, and Hayley had a horrible feeling that if he was buried, he was buried alive. The reason for the amnesia could be that he had suffered a brain trauma before he passed. Lillian would be the best one to know if that was possible.

"Call me Bones. The others do."

"Well, just until we find out your real name. I can't do much today because I'm here with a friend to get fit for a mini-marathon. But luckily for you, I know some other spirits that can help. They run The Deadly Detective Agency, if you've heard of them."

"I haven't heard anything for years. Although things did improve when the aerobics classes started," said Bones, smiling. Hayley just hoped he hadn't been watching her. That wouldn't have been nice for him, with all her creaking joints. She had even blown off on one particular move when she had to bring both legs up to her chin.

"I should imagine that would help, yes. What I'll do is tell my spirit friend, Abigail, and bring her over to talk to you. She's great at solving mysteries. I'm not sure when it will be, but knowing her, she'll be dying—well, wanting—to be here as soon as possible. Do you have any idea who would do that to you?"

"No idea at all. And I really just want my family to have my body and be able to bury me. I'm hoping I do have a family and friends who cared. Until I've got peace for them, I can't have any for myself."

"That's so sweet of you, Bones. I feel a bit mean calling you that."

"Don't worry about it. It's what they all call me." He pointed over to an old cedar tree where two peasants from bygone days were sitting.

"I don't know how I'm going to actually dig up the bones. Do you know exactly where they are?"

"I do. You're sitting on them!"

While Hayley was at the hotel, Lydia was at the Gorebridge Police Station. Her father had dropped her off outside. He offered to go in with her, but she felt that she could speak more freely, and moreover lie, if she was on her own.

There were two people waiting on chairs, but no one at the desk. So she braced herself and asked if she could see Sergeant Dave Mills as Hayley had suggested. He asked for her name and picked up the phone. When asked, Lydia told him it was about the murder of her mother, Penelope Aston-Whyte.

After fifteen long minutes, a scruffy-looking man in a shiny grey suit came out from a door to her left. She had imagined he would look a lot younger and kinder than this one.

"Ms Aston-Whyte?"

"Yes, that's me. Are you Sergeant Mills?"

"No. He's not here at the moment, love. You'll have to make do with me. I'm his senior officer, Detective Chief Inspector Johnson of CID. What's all this about a murder? I had a quick look at the report, and my men put it down as an accident."

"It wasn't an accident; it was murder, Inspector."

"Oi, Ted. Put an APB out. Suspect is about eighteen inches tall, four legs, green eyes, wearing a fur coat and goes by the name of Tibbles. He obviously planned the whole thing." Johnson and the desk sergeant both laughed. Lydia didn't.

"I don't think you should be making light of my mother's death."

"Quite right, love. I apologise. But from what I can tell, she went up the ladder and lost her balance. Should've got a man to do it. End of."

"What would you say if I told you that she said she was being followed and was scared for her life?"

"I'd say, give me proof. Have you got a suspect? Or a reason why anyone would be after her, or want to hurt her? Unless Tibbles didn't like his tinned food."

Lydia ignored that, trying to keep her voice from trembling. "No, she didn't say who was following her. That's up to you to find out."

"I won't have a slip of a girl telling me my job, thank you. In fact, you're probably the only suspect, unless you've got a sibling. You stand to gain a good bit of money and a nice house in Becklesfield that's probably worth near on a million."

"Don't be ridiculous. Why would I come and tell you to look into the murder if I did it?"

"Maybe you know the evidence or the autopsy will point to something, and you're hedging your bets. It wouldn't be the first time."

Lydia began to wish that she hadn't come. "Well, I'll expect an apology when you find out the truth."

"I wouldn't hold my breath, love. Just go home, sweetheart, and arrange the funeral or something. Leave it to the big boys to sort out the evidence. Oh, and look out for the killer cat." He looked over at Ted behind the desk and rolled his eyes as he passed him.

Lydia didn't know whether to cry or swear. But she knew that she felt even more determined to prove that her mother was murdered.

Chapter 6

IN THE SAME CORNER OF THE CRICKETERS AS BEFORE, another meeting was taking place to discuss the campathon.

Melody Myatt started the proceedings after the drinks had been bought. She had Penelope's folder on her lap after collecting it from Lydia. "First of all, I want to say how sad I am about the accidental death of our friend and colleague, Penelope. But her good work must go on, and I hope you will support me, as Race Director, to make sure that the event goes ahead." There was a murmur of assent, and then Melody carried on. "Also, I'd like to welcome Caroline to our group, who kindly agreed to start the race, and is also taking part. So welcome, Lady Caroline Hatton."

"Thank you, Melody. And I'm so sorry about Penelope. I didn't know her very well, but I know how hard she worked for her charity. So I'm glad I can help. Please let me know if you want me to do anything else."

"You might live to regret saying that, love," said Harvey Bonson. "Look at me. A few sausages, they said."

"Not this again," said Sebastian. "Get over it. You'll die a rich man."

"So will you if you don't shut up, sooner than you think."

"Please, gentlemen," said Melody. "Think of all the children we're trying to help. Now, Verity, are you going to be able to manage everything at the hospital side of things?"

"Most of it is done, actually. Just a few things to sort out. Sebastian, have you ordered the portable toilets and worked out where the band is going to be?"

"Yes. I've got a company coming to build a stage two days before. Hopefully, the weather will be okay. It's not covered."

Melody said, "That's one thing we can't do anything about. Hopefully, the good Lord will make it fine."

Sebastian added, "Well, the sun shines on the righteous, apparently."

"Mebbe you'd better get yourself a roof for it then, laddie," said Harvey snidely.

The farmer decided to ignore the miserable old goat. "The grass will be mowed a few days before as well. I know we'll have tables and chairs, but I'm going to put bales of hay around for seating. And I'm getting some signs made to direct them to the car park first."

"And I'll have the meat ready. I'll get my men to bring it in one of the cold vans on the day. The firm I use for the hire of the barbecues is paid and ready. By me, I might add."

"Thank you, Harvey," said Melody. "I've heard from our surprise group as well. I think you'll be pleased. They will be the last band on, probably about nine o'clock for an hour. We're very honoured."

"I know Penelope wouldn't, but can't you tell us who they are?" asked Verity.

"No. She made a promise, and if it got out, we'd be inundated with their fans, and then you'd have to get more meat, Harvey."

"In that case, keep it to yourself, love. I probably wouldn't have heard of them anyway."

Sebastian sniggered. "That's true. It's not going to be a group from the fifties."

Caroline quickly tried to change the subject. "Please let me order us all another round." They all thought that was the best idea yet.

After Caroline had taken a large gulp of her gin and tonic, she said, "Between us, I heard through a friend that Penelope's fall might have been an attack rather than an accident."

"Rubbish, er, sorry, Lady Caroline," said Harvey. "Twere an accident. Silly woman climbed up a ladder to save a bloomin' cat. Women shouldn't be climbing ladders."

Verity snapped, "Don't be ridiculous. A woman can climb a ladder as well as any man."

"Well, obviously not," Harvey replied.

"I'm with Verity; of course we can. But I was definitely told that someone pushed her, though I'm not sure why."

"First I've heard of it," said Sebastian. "Who would want to kill poor Penelope? You can't just say that."

"It's only what I was told in confidence. I thought you should know. The police might look into it more and want to talk to you."

"Although, she could rub people up the wrong way," agreed Verity. "There are a few I could mention at the hospital who couldn't stand her. She made a lot of money, but she was very adamant about how they should spend it. And she liked everyone to know it was all down to her. She could be very controlling at times. I even heard someone say that she didn't always give all that was collected to the hospitals either."

Melody nodded in agreement. "She was always on at me to do this, do that. Usually when I already had. But I can't imagine her keeping any of the money for herself. Although, thinking about it, there was a maternity ward somewhere that was missing some equipment she had promised. But I was very fond of her, for all that."

Sebastian said to Harvey, "Nothing would surprise me anymore. Charity begins at home, and she was never short of money. Well, look how she got us donating, Harvey. I only agreed to the field, and look at all the extras she pinned on me."

"Ain't that the truth. 'Just a few sausages', she said. Sausages; my ar... eye."

Lady Caroline noted how quickly the talk had gone from a much-loved colleague to a person they believed was greedy, dishonest, overbearing, and could easily have been pushed to her death.

Back in Church Lane, a tired Hayley had received a phone call from Lydia to say she had been to Gorebridge Police Station, and so she said she would go round to see her straight away. It was only a ten-minute walk across to the other side of the village, so Hayley thought about having a bit of a jog but decided to walk. She was tempted to take the car but decided it wouldn't be very green. She was still sore from her time at the gym. She arrived to see Roary on the front step and felt a pang of sympathy, wondering if the cat knew what his actions had caused. Was he even sitting there waiting for his mum to come home? Hayley would have liked to tell him that murderers are like water; they find a stream to escape eventually. But he looked unruffled, as he nonchalantly licked a paw and rubbed it on his pink nose.

Next door, Mrs Boyes shouted, "Arthur, Arthur, she's back again. And talking to the cat. I always thought she was a witch."

Dr Boyes sighed and carried on reading his book. "Who's back?"

"That Moon woman, the psychic. I told you Lydia's up to something. She moved in there fast enough. The body wasn't even cold."

"She's entitled to live there, so come away."

"I haven't seen the brother come yet. He was an odd boy.

The husband came fast enough, but even he's gone now. He can't have been too upset. Remember how they used to argue? I felt sorry for him, having to live with her. I wish I knew what was going on in there."

"You need a psychic," he said sarcastically.

Lydia opened the door and stood aside to let Hayley in. Hayley took in her puffy, red eyes but also sensed anger. "Dad gave me a lift there, and I saw DCI Johnson. I asked for that Sergeant Mills, but he wasn't there, so Johnson came out. Laughed to start with. He shouted to the policeman behind the desk to put out an APB on a suspect. About eighteen inches, four legs, green eyes, and goes by the name of Tibbles, as he'd obviously planned the whole thing. And then when I didn't laugh at his joke, he almost arrested me! Said that I was the only one with a motive, as I stood to gain a house and her money. I said, then why would I have gone to tell him that it wasn't an accident? He said I was covering my tracks in case the autopsy showed something different."

"I'm so sorry you had to go through that, hun. I wouldn't blame you if you didn't say any more about it."

"No, I owed it to Mum. I was an awful teenager, so this can make amends for all the times I was a little brat to her."

"Most of us were, hun. It's part of the job."

"But I was a real cow. It was about the time that they divorced, so I took it out on Mum and blamed her, even though I knew Dad could be horrible to her sometimes. And I know she didn't want me to move out, but I left anyway. I wish I could go back in time. So I owed her and totally lied to Johnson, Hayley, and said that last time I saw Mum, she said someone had been following her and she feared for her life. Even then he said he had enough cases without some slip of a girl wasting his time, and if I wanted to blame someone, I should get rid of the cat. He said he'd believe a doctor, not me."

"Well done for trying anyway. We won't give up, though.

Your mother is here, by the way. And she says there was nothing you ever did that would make her stop loving you. And she's so proud you went to see the police for her. She knows how hard it was for you."

"That's alright, Mum. I'm just sorry I failed. Dad says I can stay there if I like, but I'd rather be here to look after Roary. But if he gets on the roof, he can forget it. I did find the stuff Mum said about, like the money behind the mirror. I really needed that. I'm not going back to work for a while. They've agreed to give me a few weeks off, but I hated working there. Maybe I won't have to now. And I found the will in the bureau. And I tell you what started me crying—I found an envelope with her memories of me. There was a lock of my hair, drawings I'd done from as far back as nursery, certificates I'd won at sports day, and every single Mother's Day card I'd made for her. There were a few things for my brother, but mostly it was mine."

"She must have really loved you, Lydia. So you can't have been that bad. I'm sure she would have understood the problem you had with the divorce. Mums know these things, and they soon forget."

"I'm so glad I have the chance to say I'm sorry and that I love her," Lydia sobbed.

"She loves you, and she knows you'll have the strength to carry on. But first, we need to find out who killed her. They may have just meant to hurt her, of course."

"It's an awful feeling to know that someone hated her enough to hurt her."

"It may not be anything that personal. Penelope could have been in the wrong place at the wrong time. There could be a lot of scenarios. Did your father have any ideas?"

"Nothing. He's in shock too. That policeman said me and my brother are the only suspects. Let's hope he has an alibi."

"I was just wondering, Lydia, where were you when she died?"

"Great, even you think I'm guilty."

"Of course I don't, but the police will want to know if they start an investigation, so it's best to be prepared."

"I arrived a bit before the ambulance. Dr Boyes can verify that. I had left work early and decided to visit. The truth was I didn't fancy going back to my flat. At least Mum had nice food in her cupboards."

"Hmm. He heard the crash and came out, so you must have been close. The ambulance didn't take long to come. The police will need to know exactly where you were when she fell. Where were you before that?"

"I left work early. I wish I hadn't now. I drove straight here and parked outside on the road. I suppose someone saw me pull up and get out of the car. I bet old Mrs Boyes was looking."

"Apparently she wasn't, much to her annoyance. But I expect Dr Boyes heard you arrive, so don't worry. Is your brother coming?"

"Calum, yes. As soon as he's sorted out the dog. I told him he didn't have to bring Vanessa, but that annoyed him."

"Don't you like her, then?"

"Not a lot. Nor did Mum. They clashed. It was more the way she talked down to Calum. She spends his money like water as well."

"Have you opened the will yet, Lydia?"

"Yes, I did. I'm well taken care of. There's a note to say that I should ring her solicitor, which I'll probably do tomorrow."

"I know there's this house, but do you think she will have left a lot of money?"

"Not a fortune, but quite a lot. She got quite a bit in the divorce, and Nanny and Gramps passed away in the last few years, so she got their money and a half share of their house with her sister. Oh my God, I haven't told her sister. How awful am I?"

"Not at all. You're trying your best. Would you like me to phone her?"

"No, it's okay. I've got Auntie Bridget's number on my phone. I'll do it when you've gone."

Hayley stood up. "I'll let you get on then. Ring me if you need me, hun. And well done for going to the police station. I really hope the police open a murder inquiry. I might even do something myself."

Hayley said goodbye and went outside to look where Penelope had once laid, followed by the victim herself.

"You're going, aren't you, Penelope?" said Hayley gently.

"Yes, I'm going. I feel I must. Lydia and her brother need to grieve and move on. Besides, it's not right, my being here. It doesn't feel natural."

"Some would say it's supernatural. But I understand."

"I've done what I needed to do, and I have faith that the guilty will pay. Tell her goodbye and say I've gone to be with Gramps and Nanny. She'll understand. Thank you, Hayley."

Hayley nodded and wished Penelope well as she walked away and disappeared.

"Arthur, Arthur. She's outside now. And she's talking to herself."

"Who?"

"That strange Hayley Moon woman, of course."

Dr Boyes shook his head, and thought he knew who was the stranger of the two.

Hayley went home as fast as her aching bones would move, looking forward to Tom telling her that they were going to open a murder enquiry.

"Sorry, Hayl, they aren't going to open a murder enquiry."

"You're kidding, Tom. I can't believe it. Why the hell not?"

"Nothing in the postmortem to support it. Penelope Aston-

Whyte was over fifty, up a ladder, and had been to the pub where she'd drunk at least three large white wines."

"It's not like she was over seventy, for goodness' sake. Fifty is nothing these days. Or are they saying it's because she's a woman?"

"More that the blood alcohol in her system was eighty-five milligrams of alcohol per one hundred millilitres of blood. And the fact that she had court shoes on. She couldn't have driven, put it that way. The inquest will be a while, but I'm sure the coroner will rule it an accidental death. Sorry, Hayl."

"I'm not looking forward to telling Abigail and the others. Perhaps we can find a motive and a suspect."

"Apart from her children, you mean."

"Yes, that's the trouble. Penelope wouldn't want to get her children in trouble. That would backfire on her, especially if it turns out it was one of them, or the daughter-in-law. Is there anything you can do to help, Tom?"

"Not unless Johnson says so. I could possibly make a few enquiries at the other houses in Bellringer Close, and have another look around, but that's about it. Sorry, you're on your own, so be careful."

"At the meeting for the fun run, Caroline found out that she wasn't quite the popular, thoughtful fundraiser that we thought. She could be rather persuasive and bossy and run roughshod over everyone."

"Sounds like someone we know."

Hayley laughed. "Yes, Abigail. And I rest my case. Look what happened to her – murdered. There was even a suggestion that she may have kept some of the raised money for herself. It was Verity Pikestaff from the hospital who first brought that up. And changing the subject, I've got to tell you something very important."

"You're pregnant!"

"No! I would have told you that first, I promise. It doesn't always happen straight away. But it will happen, hun." Hayley was rather relieved. She wasn't sure how ready she was to have a baby. The cat was enough trouble. But Tom was so excited at the thought of being a father that she had agreed to try when he had suggested it. And although she sensed that both of their children were going to be as psychic and spiritually gifted as she was, she didn't see herself expecting anytime soon.

"What is it then? Don't tell me there's another murderer on the loose."

"Close, but no, nothing like that, hun. I simply want to know how easy it is to dig up a dead body!"

Chapter 7

"Honestly, you would have thought I asked him something difficult," shrugged Hayley.

Terry sighed, "I do feel for poor old Tom. What other husband has to go through this?"

"So can you go and get a shovel and just start digging?" asked Abigail.

"No, I can't, unfortunately. If it was in my back garden I probably could, but not in the grounds of a hotel."

"What about the owners? Could we ask them?"

"Maybe, but it would take a lot of explaining, and I'm not even a member of the spa. I hate asking Caroline for favours, so we need to think of something else. The owner is an American lady, Tom said."

"Terry and I could go and have a look around. Get an idea of what she's like."

"Good idea, Abigail." Terry loved it when just the two of them went on an investigation.

"Wouldn't hurt. I didn't see her when I went. Let me look online for her details." Hayley picked up her phone and started tapping.

"I'm absolutely amazed you can find out on that," said Terry. "In my day, you'd have to... well, I don't know how you could ever find that out."

"Here we are. Just like that, Terry, I can tell you that Courtridge Castle was bought by Maria Dubois in 2020. It was built in the 12th century by Henry II and was little more than ruins. Blah blah. It's now a five-star hotel and spa, set on fifty acres. She is the only daughter of seventies rock star, Dirk Dubois, of the rock group, Dark Brethren. I was not expecting that. Maria has been married to Anita Diaz since 2022."

"Well, I was not expecting that," said Terry.

"Live and let love, Terry. Look at us. Times have moved on, thank goodness."

Terry said, "Love is love," and winked at Abigail. "Who would have thought that you and I would get together. We're like chalk and cheese."

"I wouldn't say we're that different. I'm more like a fine Brie and you're like a well-matured cheddar."

"Cheese and wine is always better when it's well-matured. Is there a picture of her?" asked Terry. "Oh, very nice. Yes, I think we should definitely go and have a good look at the Courtridge. I remember her dad's group, Dark Brethren. He was English, but went over to California and stayed there. I had one of their 78s."

"What on earth is a 78?" asked Abigail.

"Really? You don't know what a 78 is? What about a 45?"

"Ah, that I do know. It's a bullet, or a gun."

"We come from different worlds. They're records. There's so much you youngsters don't know," Terry said with a sigh.

"So, clever clogs, what is an app?"

"An app is an, um..."

Hayley cleared her throat. "If I can carry on, you two, you need to go and see what they're like. And see if you find anything out that could help us to get to that body. That poor boy needs to rest in peace."

Abigail nodded. "You mean so we can blackmail them."

"No, I don't! Abigail Summers, how could you even think of that?"

"It was quite easy."

"Why don't you go as well, Betty. Keep those two on the straight and narrow."

"I'd love to go to a spanky hotel." Betty had a habit of getting words wrong as well as her sayings.

"I think you mean swanky," said Abigail.

"Oh no, you have your hobbies and my John and I had ours," Betty said with a twinkle in her eye.

Hayley and the others laughed. "Your John was a lucky man, for sure. So I just want to know if she's approachable. If not, I don't know what we'll do."

"Don't worry," said Abigail. "I've got a few ideas. One or two of them might even be legal."

That evening, as the sun was going down, the three spirits, Terry, Betty, and Abigail, walked up the long driveway to the Courtridge Hotel and Spa. The couple held hands and both felt sadness that they were dead and not able to check in and enjoy a stay themselves. Betty, on the other hand, was delighted that she was having the experience and it wasn't costing her a penny. John would never have agreed to coming somewhere as expensive as this. More money than sense, he would have said, thought Betty.

Usually they walked in any entrance unnoticed, but for some reason the automatic double doors opened as they approached.

Terry smiled. "Well, there you go. Part of us must still be here. The sensors picked us up."

"It's rather nice to be noticed for a change, instead of being literally a nobody," said Betty.

Abigail said, "As long as we aren't charged. I wonder how much it costs for the night. Look at the size of the front desk. What I noticed in life, the fancier the reception, the better the hotel."

And this was the most opulent that she had ever seen. It was the size of a tennis court and had leather sofas and coffee tables all around the room in front of six-foot original paintings. The ceiling was as high as a church, and a grand chandelier marked the centre. The American owner, Maria Dubois, had obviously pastiched the London hotels of the 1930s that were frequented by the rich and famous of the world. A man in a black suit was checking in a guest, as a bellboy waited with her luggage on a brass trolley.

"Shall we have a look around before we find Maria and Anita? We're only assuming they live here. Maybe they live somewhere else. Or they might have gone back to America," said Abigail.

"Ooh, yes, we must. I've waited all my life to come somewhere like this, although we did have a week in Eastbourne in a hotel for our fiftieth wedding anniversary. Had a sea view and everything, but it was nothing like here."

"I would have liked the spa, Betty," said Abigail. "I was going to go for a pamper weekend for my fortieth birthday, but fate and a cold-blooded killer meant that I never did."

"At least you'll never get to be forty, dear. You know what they say, 'Nobody loves a fairy when she's forty.'"

"Do they really? I wonder why?"

Terry said, "Even I know that. It was a song, I think."

"That's right, dear, it was, I remember now. How did it go? 'Nobody loves a fairy when she's forty, Nobody loves a fairy when she's old. Her magic's not enough. They want a younger bit of stuff,'" Betty sang.

Abigail and Terry realised that Betty's singing skills were on the same level as her sayings knowledge.

Terry said, "Well, as you two are always telling me, you can't say that these days. It's ageist to fairies."

"And definitely sexist," agreed Abigail, with a wink at him. "I really think we should get on and see what's what and if the owner is here."

Betty didn't seem to notice they were trying to stop her singing and said, "Hayley had a feeling they would be here, and she's usually right. I bet they've got private quarters somewhere."

"Would you ladies like to accompany me to the dining room?" said Terry, holding out both his arms.

They needn't have worried about Maria not being there, as they heard an American accent. "I'm so glad that you enjoyed your meal, Mrs Ponsenby. Our chef is French, you know. Don't forget our bar serves some wonderful cocktails. Please have one on us."

Abigail said to Terry, "She's making a fortune. Feeds them all these calories at night, and then charges them hundreds of pounds to take the weight off the next day."

"I never used to put any weight on, whatever I ate," he replied.

"I did," said Betty. "But I didn't care. When I was young, if you were skinny, you were poor, and likely to get rickets or scurvy."

"That's true, Betty. I remember those days too. Even as I got older, I couldn't put on weight if I wanted to."

Abigail rolled her eyes. "Well, aren't you the lucky one? I liked chocolate too much. I was an addict; there, I've admitted it."

That gave Betty a chance to say one of her sayings. "Remember, a bit on your lips is an inch on your hips. No, that doesn't sound right either. An inch on your lips is a pinch on your waist.

No, not an inch, it's a minute and something on your hips. Or is it a lifetime?"

"It certainly feels like it," murmured Abigail.

"Cheeky monkey. You know you'd miss my words of wisdom if I didn't share these things with you."

"I'm sorry, Betty. You know I love you, don't you?"

"I know, dear. And you look fine to me."

"It actually took a lot of work to get this figure."

"You look just perfect to me. I never did like skinny birds," said Terry.

"Terry Styles, you can't call women birds these days."

"Why not? Birds are lovely."

"I'm not sure, but women don't like it."

"Okay, crumpet, or dolly birds," joked Terry. "I know, I can't say that either. People have got very fussy these days. We meant birds in a very complimentary way. So I can't say my bird looks ravishing, or a stunner, or a knockout?"

"I might make an exception for that, just this once. But all I can say is it's a good job you're dead." They followed Mrs Ponsenby into the large art deco bar. Abigail carried on, "So tell me about these birds."

"In the sixties, if you were lucky, you'd pick up a bird on the Friday and go out on the Saturday. If you were very lucky, you'd stay in," said Terry with a cheeky grin.

"Oh yeah? And how often were you lucky?"

"Not as lucky as I would have liked to be, if I'm honest."

"Once? Twice?"

"I had my moments. You wouldn't have been able to keep away, Abigail, that I do know."

"I'd have been too busy myself on a Saturday night. Well, once or twice."

Betty joined in. "Me and my John could get lucky as many times a week as we wanted. And as you know, my John wanted to get lucky a lot. Especially on a Saturday morning when…"

Abigail said quickly, "Let's go and check out the spa. See what all the fuss is about. It was on my bucket list to go in a sauna. Pity I kicked it before. Mind you, so was jumping out of a plane and swimming with sharks, so I'm not sorry about that."

"The more I know about you, the more you surprise me. Why would anyone want to swim with sharks and jump out of a plane?"

"It's very fashionable these days, Terry."

"It sure is a strange world now." They followed the signs to the gym, where there was a line of women and men on bikes.

"See what I mean?" said Terry. "Pedalling away and not going anywhere. What's wrong with going out in the country? And look at him on a rowing machine. Saves getting wet, I suppose."

"You have to keep up with progress, Terry," said Abigail as they walked out. "It's not really that strange." But then they entered one of the treatment rooms.

"You were saying?" asked Terry. Two women were lying on tables and were covered in what looked like mud, although none of them were sure what it was.

"This is… er, good for the pores."

"Might be good for dog's paws, but for goodness' sake, don't tell me they charge you for this."

"Probably about a hundred pounds, Terry."

"So you can't call them birds, but you can cover them in mud."

"Only if they want you to. Oh, what the hell, life is mad these days. Let's go and have a look at the swimming pool. That can't have changed that much since your days."

"I only went to a pool once and that was outside, and I swear there was ice on the top. I went to an old quarry once, and if you were in there any longer than five minutes, your legs would stop working. It's no wonder I never learned to swim. No kids could in our day. Wow. But if our pool was like this, I would've given it a go."

The swimming area looked like it had been built by the gods of Olympus, Abigail thought. There were tall pillars and a jacuzzi. White loungers were around the edge and the water sparkled like stars. Abigail had to nudge Terry in the ribs to get him to take his eyes off two girls who were standing by the edge wearing bikinis.

"Maybe some things have changed for the better. I take it all back."

"Oh yes, I forget in your days women used to wear those all-in-one, frilly bathing suits that went down to their ankles."

"Now don't be like that, you daft mare. You're still my bird," Terry said and gave her one of his smiles that lit up his handsome but rugged face. Abigail even felt proud to be his bird.

She started to leave, "Let's go and find Maria. That is why we're here, don't forget. It's not to look at young women. They must live in some private quarters somewhere." As the words left her lips, a rather well-muscled young man in tight trunks walked in with a towel over his shoulder. "On the other hand, we could stay a bit longer, Betty. There's really no rush."

"Abigail Summers, stop staring. That's not the private quarters we're after. And you, Betty. Honest to goodness."

"What? I was just thinking we had towels like that. I hadn't even noticed the man in his red swimming speedos!" said Betty.

"Exactly. Men gawp; us ladies, glance. As a dressmaker, I was merely making a professional observation that he needs a slightly larger size of swimming trunks. Don't you agree, Betty?"

"Actually, I think they are the perfect size. And the trunks," she chuckled.

"And I can't say birds," sighed Terry. "Come on, put your eyes back in their sockets, ladies. Let's go."

They found a door between the stairs and the lift marked 'Private. No Entry', but not for the three ghosts who walked through unseen by the guests in the lobby. So they decided to see if that was where they would find the owner and her wife. Terry and Abigail were expecting stairs to lead to a flat, but there was a lift which was not for use by staff.

"Well that's torn it," said Terry. "If we go in, how can we press the button to go up? If only Suzie was here. She'd be able to do it. The lift might not even be there. It could still be on another floor."

"There's only one way to find out." Abigail put her head through the metal sliding door. "Nope, not even there. We could go up the stairs, but we don't know what floor they live on. Let's go and see if Maria is still down here and follow her. If not, we'll just have to search the whole hotel."

Luckily for them, Maria was still being the perfect hostess and working the restaurant. They thought she seemed very pleasant, but that could be because they were paying over the top for the privilege of staying there.

"I mean, Abi, look at the size of the meals. If they served that tiny little bit of food in the middle of that big plate, they'd have a riot at a pub. Is that cheesecake with a bit of sauce drizzled on? I'd get that in my mouth in one mouthful."

"Terry, Terry, Terry. Don't you know that the posher the restaurant, the smaller the meal?" Abigail said, shaking her head.

"Why? I would have thought the more you're paying, the bigger the meal. So why?"

"Er, it's to look better on the plate perhaps. I don't know. It's just the way it is, Terry."

"Seems like slim pickings to me. That old boy has got less cheese on his plate than I'd put on my mouse traps."

"And that's why you don't know about these things," Abigail laughed.

"The rich get rich, and the poor get poorer," sighed Terry. "And thinner, by the looks of it."

"I'm with you, Terry," said Betty. "John liked meat and two veg, every day. Except on a Friday. That was fish and chips day."

"See. Betty knows what I mean. You had to eat when you could in our day."

"Oh, boohoo, Oliver Twist. You didn't do that bad." Abigail then remembered that Terry had been brought up in an orphanage. It was only when Abigail herself had looked into it that he found out that he did have a family. She felt a bit guilty and said, "Sorry, darling, I forgot about your childhood." And she kissed him on his cheek. Terry loved that she had called him darling and given him a kiss. But more than that, she had acknowledged that he had had a bad start to life. No one else ever had, especially when he was alive.

"That's alright, love. I'm happy now, and that's all that matters."

Betty said, "The food does look good. It's called Cord and Blue, you know. I expect they've got Michelin tyres as well."

"Michelin stars, I think you mean."

"They make tyres, Abigail. Everyone knows that," Betty corrected her. "Don't worry. They say the person that never made a mistake, never made... What was it now?"

"Anything?" replied Abigail helpfully.

"Yes, it really could be anything. What was it now? Oh, it'll come back to me, dear."

Abigail thought it quicker to change the subject, and they followed Maria for a while. They all agreed that the owner of the hotel was equally nice to her staff and thought that would help if they needed to get her onboard. Abigail had never been patient and was just about to give up and leave when Maria Dubois told the head waiter that she was going up for the night. They followed her on her way to her room.

"At last," said Terry. "I thought she'd never leave. Keep up, Abigail. If we miss the lift, we've had it."

"I'm coming. And they say I'm bossy."

"You are," he answered seriously, as Maria pressed for the lift and it silently descended. She wrapped her arms around herself and shivered at a drop in temperature inside the lift. There was only one button, and that had four on it, so Terry, Betty, and Abigail guessed that Maria and Anita must live in the penthouse suite. Although, since it was once a castle, it was more likely to be the turret room. When the lift door opened, the thick carpet of the rest of the hotel was replaced by a stone floor. Maria came to a door and slipped in a keycard to open it.

"What's that?" asked Terry. "Don't tell me they've got rid of keys as well."

"It's like a key. It's got a strip on it that clicks the door open. I don't know how. But keys are so last century, Terry," joked Abigail.

"No more keys, no proper meals. I really despair sometimes. Why can't…." Terry stopped his usual crusade on the future of mankind when Anita came to the door and gave her wife a kiss on the lips and a hug. "I never said a word," said Terry as Abigail turned around to look at him, as he had a big smile on his face. "You know me, I'm all for progress."

"Good. We've got enough on our plate."

"Unlike the people in the restaurant," added Terry. "So what are we looking for exactly?" They took in the sitting room, which was very unlike the opulence of the rest of the hotel. The furniture was more bargain basement than penthouse. Maybe the two Americans weren't that well off.

"I have no idea. I suppose we'll know when we find it. Not that we can use it against them, according to Hayley. Maybe we just need to find an excuse for her to pay them a visit and nonchalantly say, 'Oh, by the way, you've got a murder victim buried under a bench in your garden'. But then add that they can't tell the police because DCI Johnson will go mad if the info comes from her."

"Perhaps they're interested in history and she could tell them that there's a Roman villa on the grounds."

"They don't look like the type to me." Anita was dressed more casually than her suited partner. "Let's have a listen."

Maria had flopped on the sofa, and Anita turned off the television and sat down opposite her. "You're late. I suppose it's good we're busy. See, things are starting to turn around."

"I know, but we need it to be like this all the time. The health spa is doing okay. It helps that a lot have taken out a membership for the gym to get fit for the fun run. Not that they'll carry on coming afterwards, but at least they will have paid the fee. That should shut the bank up for a while."

"Your dad is coming over in a few weeks. He's always saying how much royalties he gets from the band's music catalogue. He'd love to help, sweetheart."

"I know. But I don't want to ask him for any more though. He lent me the money as an investment, and I'm damn sure I'm going to pay him back every last cent. Or rather penny."

"You said we might have to sell if things don't change. Surely it's better to ask him than lose everything. What's he coming for, did he say?"

"Not really. Some kind of surprise. He's getting together with old friends and his bandmates from Dark Brethren. Although some have died."

"So how about doing some weekend events? Like the 80s. They can be very popular. Maybe he could make an appearance."

"I don't think so, Anita. Doesn't really go with the look I'm after."

"A murder mystery weekend then. You could have Lady Phillipa Fontainebleu kill the Marquis de Foofoo or something."

Maria sat forward. "Actually I love it. We could do one a month. I've no idea how, but I bet there's a firm we could get in with actors and a whodunit story. Brilliant idea. Keep going while you're on a roll."

"A casino weekend. Er, or even better a psychic weekend. With readings and tarot cards and so on."

"I love the idea of that. We could do a ghost hunt in the hotel and give a talk about the murderous deeds that happened when it was a castle. If only it was haunted. We've never seen a shadow, let alone a ghost," sighed Maria.

Abigail smiled and shook her head. "If only they knew, Terry."

"You can say that again, madam," said a disembodied voice, as the bedroom door slowly opened.

Chapter 8

BETTY AND ABIGAIL GRABBED EACH OTHER, AND Terry stepped in front of them, then demanded whoever it was should show themselves if they knew what was good for them.

"As it's my castle, I suggest it's you who should be introducing yourselves."

Abigail stepped out from behind Terry. "Please excuse us. You caught us unawares."

"You're forgiven, young lady. It's a while since I've had visitors. Sir Timothy Whittlebury at your service," he said with a bow. He looked to be in his sixties and was dressed in a white shirt with wide sleeves and a brown waistcoat, with matching breeches.

"I'm Abigail and this is Betty, and this is our protector, Terry Styles."

"Welcome to Courtridge Castle. As I was going to say, I've been doing my best to haunt those two, and do they notice? Nothing. It takes all my energy to open that door, and they simply remark on how there's a wind blowing in through the old windows."

"How frustrating for you, Sir Whittlebury," said Betty.

"Sir Timothy will suffice, my lady. It's been a long time since I saw anyone as comely as yourself," said the elderly gent, as he went over and kissed the back of her hand.

Once again, Abigail felt a bit jealous of Betty. For an old fairy, she sure could attract the men. There was Willy Morgan at the marina, she remembered. He was most hurt when she didn't go up the river with him on a date. Abigail was starting to wonder if it was because Betty was nice. Could that be the secret? She could be nice, couldn't she? Hayley was nice. Surely it couldn't be that hard. From now on, she would be the nicest and kindest ghost in Becklesfield.

Terry interrupted her epiphany. "Wake up, Dolly Daydream. Sir Timothy is talking to you."

"What?! I was thinking about something really important," she snapped. Perhaps it was harder than she thought. She'd start being nice tomorrow. "Sorry, Sir, we need to find out something about the couple that owns the hotel. Have you been here long? We died not that long ago, but Terry's been dead for about fifty years."

"He's just a boy. For more than three centuries I've walked the ramparts every night at dusk. It's where I died and where I'm cursed to stay. I don't suppose you've heard the legend of my demise, have you? No, nobody has these days. It used to be told with fear to the children, but not any longer, alas."

Abigail went into the bedroom from where the gentleman had come and sat on the four-poster bed. She patted it for the others to join her. "Please tell us, we'd be fascinated."

"Good idea. I have to hear those two chattering all day and night." He stood with his back against an unlit fireplace that filled one wall. There was a door that led out onto the top of the castle opposite him. "The legend in this area goes like this. My first wife died in childbirth with our seventh child when I was thirty, and I didn't find love again until I was forty-four. I died up here while looking out over the moors for my loved one, who had been kidnapped by my enemies. I put together an army but never found her. I died alone of a broken heart, still watching. Forced to walk on the battlements till the end of time."

"I'm so sorry, Sir Timothy. And you really died of a broken heart?" Betty asked, with her hand over her own.

"No. Actually, my new wife left me for a younger man, and the cook fed me venison that was three weeks old. I came up here and went out to get some fresh air, and then slipped on where I had been violently sick, and hit my head."

Terry and Abigail both laughed. "I can see that wouldn't have been half so interesting," she said. Betty just gave Sir Timothy a concerned look.

"Well, the circumstances of my death have long been forgotten in the folklore of the area. A shame, but there it is. No one has heard of Sir Timothy Whittlebury. Let alone that he haunts the castle."

"That might be about to change," said Abigail. "Do you know what a medium is?"

Sir Timothy rubbed his beard thoughtfully. "Hmm. In the days of yore, it meant something was smaller than a big, and bigger than a small."

"But if we are referring to a person."

"Same thing, I suppose. Look, what is all this about?" he asked Terry, thinking that women's brains had not got better over the years.

"A medium is a person who can talk to the dead. We have a friend who can see them as well and gets feelings."

"Oh, you mean a witch. We had many of those in our days. I had about twenty executed myself."

Abigail was furious. "No, we do not mean a witch! And that did not give you the right to kill all those women just because they had gifts. I bet most of them were handed over to the authorities because there wasn't such a thing as divorce in those days. Anyway, our friend, Hayley, helps everyone with kindness and love. She is definitely not a witch."

"Does she predict the future?"

"Yes, sometimes."

"Does she heal the sick with potions and touch?"

"Well, yes."

"Talk to the dead?"

"All the time, but…"

"Does she sense danger?"

"On occasion."

"Does she curse your very soul to hell if you slight her?"

"No, definitely not."

Sir Timothy folded his arms. "She sounds like a witch to me, and as such should be at the very least drowned till she's dead."

Terry tried to defuse the situation. "Sir, things have changed even since I was alive. We have to move with the times, as I'm always being told. Witches are no longer persecuted, and actually, women are thought of as equals to men."

Sir Timothy scoffed. "Now that I will never believe. So, what do you want here?" he said impatiently.

Abigail decided to take a softer approach. After all, he was over three hundred years old, and her mother had always told her to respect the elderly. "Our friend, Hayley, is trying to help one of the other ghosts at the castle. Do you know a young man who was buried on the grounds by the lake?"

"You must mean Bones. A very nice young man."

"Yes, that's him. He's asked Hayley to discover who killed him, so his family can have closure. He can't remember who they are, and that's where we come in. We are private detectives who get to the truth."

"Do you mean like witchfinders?"

"Oh, don't start that again, please," said Abigail. "No, I mean like the police. Did you have any lawmen in your day?"

"We had officers of the law. But around here, that would have been me," he said proudly.

"The only thing is, that to investigate, we need to be able to get at the body. Hopefully, legally, and keep all the evidence intact. But to do that, we need to get the permission of the owner."

"You have my permission and best wishes."

"Ah, thank you. But I was actually thinking of the current owner, Maria Dubois, I'm sorry to say."

"Of course, of course. So how can I help?"

"We just heard that they might be forced to sell Courtridge if they don't make some more money, and they want to do a supernatural weekend. Now, this would mean that Hayley could help out and show them that she's not a fake. And I was just thinking that you could tell her where all the best ghosts were for the ghost hunt. And the stories behind them. We would be so grateful, Sir."

"Well, I would like to be of some use. Let's see. Well, to start with, there's the ghost of the cook that gave me the three-week-old venison. He was put to death the next day, of course."

"Of course," said Hayley, giving Terry a quick glance.

"There were a few other beheadings and hangings. Some were nothing to do with me. Then there's Jock the Scot. You'll find him in the great hall. He's the one in a kilt and a dirk in his stomach. Nancy, the maid, is usually in the kitchen. Well, it used to be the kitchen. It's where the hypnotherapy pool is now, whatever that is. There's Boris the executioner. He was executed himself in the end. I'd say there's about twenty ghosts inside and more outside. Plenty in the dungeon, although they call it the wine cellar now."

"It was rather brutal in those days," said Betty.

"No more than it is now. In the daytime, I still walk the main halls. You'd be surprised at what I see. They have their own torture chambers here. In one of the rooms, they practise 'death of a thousand needles'. A man, and sometimes a woman, sticks pins in their backs and even in their faces. Even I never condoned that."

"That's acupuncture."

"I don't know what an acu is, but it was definitely punctured. Then there's a torture where they put hot wax on bodies. On legs and also somewhere I can't mention in front of Lady Betty, and they rip it off to screams. There's even a fire room. Full of smoke and steam, where they are left till they can't breathe, and they go as red as a tree in autumn. But I agree to meet this witch of yours and tell her what I know."

"Splendid," said Betty. "We can't thank you enough, Sir Timothy."

"You can call me Timothy. Would you care to accompany me on my walk on the battlements tonight, m'lady?"

"Well, I can honestly say I've never had a proposition like that before. But I fear I will have to say no. I'm already spoken for. My husband, John, is waiting."

He kissed her hand again. "He's a lucky man, that's all I shall say."

Abigail leaned over to Terry and said, "Seriously, how does she do it?"

"She has got the X factor. Or SA as they said in my day - sex appeal."

Abigail shook her head slowly. "I was wondering, it couldn't be because she's nice, could it? Perhaps that's her secret. No wonder I never married."

"I'll never understand birds, I mean ladies. We'd better go before he starts kissing more than just her hand. Sir Timothy, that will be all for now, thank you. Could you tell us which way it is to find Bones, if we go out of the main door, please."

"Turn left at the west wing for Peasants' Path. Go down Hangman's Hill until you see Deadman's Pond, and that's where you'll find Bones' Bench."

Abigail said, "That sounds just perfect for the ghost tours of the castle. A real piece of history. We'll come back with Hayley, and you can show us all the hotspots. Or rather from past experience; cold spots."

Terry pointed out two peasants on Peasants' Path, but they didn't stop to speak, although the man and woman followed them to see what was going on. It was getting extremely dark, and luckily they didn't see anyone on Hangman's Hill. They could see Deadman's Pond because moonlight was shimmering on the surface.

"I think it should be called Deadwoman's Pond. I dread to think how many witches were drowned in it."

"It was an awful time to be a woman," said Betty. "I don't think there will be many still about. They will have gone straight to Heaven. The good Lord knew they were guilty of nothing at all. It's a good job Hayley wasn't alive in those days. Oh look, there is the young man in question."

The silhouette of a man sitting with his back to them came into view.

"Excuse me," said Terry. "Are you the one they call Bones?" A young but dirty face turned round to look at them and stood up.

"That's me. I take it that Hayley sent you."

They introduced themselves, and Bones motioned for them to take a seat on his bench. He stood in front of them. "She said that you might be able to find my murderer and my family for me."

"We're going to do our best," promised Abigail. "And we've had really good results so far. Can I ask, how come a bench just happens to be over the spot where your body was buried?"

"That was a strange thing. Above me, the grass would never grow. They did all they could, but the gardener could never understand why it would turn brown and die. I have no idea why. So they decided to put a bench here to hide it."

Terry said, "It could be fate, or it could be a chemical in your body that stopped it from growing. But for whatever reason, it's very handy. We could have been digging all over the place else."

One of the peasants spoke for the first time. "We saw it all didn't we, Bert. 'Twas dark, but 'twas a man."

"Can you describe him?"

"Nah. 'Twas dark, I tells ye."

"Sorry to be nosy," said Abigail, "But is that the rope you were hung with that you're carrying?"

"Nah, I bought it from the hangman, just before I died meself."

Betty was dying to tell them the saying that for once she got correct. "I know this one, Abigail. It's where the saying 'money for old rope' comes from. The hangman did the hanging, cut it up, and sold it after."

"Once again you amaze me, Betty."

"I'm just a pretty face, you know."

Bones wanted to get the subject back to himself. "So is that what detectives do? Dig up the body first? I've never met a private detective before. My mum used to like Porrow. Oh my God, that was a memory. My first one I've ever had since I've been here. I've got a mum."

"That's a real start," said Abigail. "Keep thinking. More might come back if you talk about it. We have to get permission from the owner first. We have a friend called Suzie that can check the newspapers in the library for that time, but I think the best thing is to go and see our friend Celia. She's a journalist for the Chiltern Weekly. Dead of course, but she has helped us with a lot of our cases. Now, she has an eidetic memory. That means she can remember anything. Names, dates, even the weather for a day in March, twenty years ago."

"The total opposite to me then."

"You could say that. Luckily for us, Celia still hangs around their offices, and we'll ask her if she can remember anything about a missing boy. Say late teens, wearing a hoodie and jeans, brown hair, hmm, about five-foot-six tall. How many years ago would you say?"

"I'm pretty sure I counted twelve winters."

"There you go then, twelve years ago. Sorted. She will say that Joe Bloggs and his family live in such and such. If we can't get permission from the police to look for your remains, the owners can. So we'll get back and start digging into it. Sorry, bad choice of words. We'll start investigating."

"You don't know how happy you've made me. Perhaps I can leave here then."

"Do you mean cross over to the other side?"

"I haven't even left the castle grounds yet. That would be a start. I was worried in case I couldn't find my way back or something would happen, so I stayed here. It's been a long, long time." As he spoke, they all turned to look where a howl had come from. On the other side of the pond, they saw a huge dog.

Abigail shivered. "Seriously, this is too spooky. How on earth can you stay here?"

"Oh, that's just Rex, the Irish Wolfhound. He still thinks he's chasing deer and wolves. He's an old softie, don't worry."

"As long as you know that you can leave if you like. We'll start and hopefully we can get you to have some fun. We have got another murder case at the moment, but we can do both at the same time. You could come to Becklesfield with us at one point. It's not far."

"I don't know the name. But it sounds like Heaven to me."

"You could even go there," Abigail promised kindly.

Chapter 9

THE FOLLOWING MORNING, HAYLEY WOKE AND stretched, then wished she hadn't. This exercising did not agree with her at all. She felt much fitter before she started working out. Now her whole body ached, and she felt worn out. She decided to stay in her warm bed a bit longer. She seemed to remember Tom kissing her head before he left for work, saying he had fed Luna, but she didn't think she had said goodbye. Where was Luna? He was unusually quiet. The tortoiseshell cat in question was on Tom's pillow. Probably not that hygienic, but what he didn't know, thought Hayley. If she lay completely still, she might be allowed a lie-in.

Luna opened one eye. Good, she was awake, about time too. It must be time for something; late breakfast or early elevenses. He went over and walked on her face, just in case she was thinking of shutting her eyes again. And to make sure, he clawed at her long, black hair. Humans could be very lazy, and he wanted his meal put in front of him sooner rather than later.

"Ouch. Yes, good morning, cat. I'm getting up any minute now. Let me think about what I'm doing today. It's alright for you, sitting around licking yourself all day."

How rude, thought Luna. He had spiders and flies to catch and scare off next door's cat through the window. Then get on the kitchen surfaces as soon as he was left on his own and make sure they were cleaned. He put his paw on her face again, and she got up at last. Owners—no, he owned them—workers could be very selfish if you didn't train them.

After Luna had his second breakfast, he took up his vigil at the conservatory window. Hayley sat on the chair next to him and started to write a list. That reminded her, she really needed to get going on writing the book about their cases. Not today, she thought. She had a reading at eleven, and at some point, she would go to the library to find out how the others got on at the hotel last night.

After the reading, where Hayley had assured a widower that his wife was safe and happy with her family, and had no problem with his selling their family home and moving to Devon, she put on her jacket and walked the short journey to the library. She had thought about jogging the long way there, but she didn't want to be late, she told herself. The others were relying on her.

Everyone was there when Hayley got to the seating at the back of the library. She had said hello to Janette, the librarian, and took a random book to pretend to read while The Deadly Detective Agency had their meeting.

Abigail was saying, "We can't just drop our other cases. There's a young boy that needs to find his family. He was buried alive. That trumps being pushed off a ladder."

Hayley said hello. "Actually, I agree with Terry. We know there is actually a murderer in the village, and for all we know, they might strike again. We're not sure what the motive was. It could be about money, and then her daughter, Lydia, might be in danger. Apparently, she and her brother are in line for an awful lot of money. I think we should do what we can for Penelope first, but also do a few things for Bones."

"Okay," said Abigail sullenly. "But as soon as we can, we need to ask Celia if she remembers a missing person's case. We might get a name then."

"Brilliant idea, hun. Before we talk about Penelope's case, I want to hear how you got on at the Courtridge Hotel last night."

"Well, Betty met another admirer," said Terry.

"There's only one for me, though, as you all know. But if I was single and alive three hundred years ago, I still wouldn't have been tempted. It was a very violent time back then. You wouldn't have liked him, Hayley. He thought you should be drowned in Deadman's Pond for witchcraft."

"No, he wouldn't be my cup of tea then." She was very impressed at all they had learned, including what they told her about Sir Timothy.

Abigail added, "But the main thing is that the hotel is in a bit of trouble financially, and they are thinking of doing event weekends. And one of the ideas was a paranormal one and a ghost tour. And Sir Timothy Whittlebury told us just where the ghosts are and will be willing to help. Gives you a great excuse to go there and help out, Hayley."

"That's marvellous, hun. I could do some readings or give a talk or something. Don't worry, it won't be until after the fun run. So what's the plan, Abigail?"

"If we're doing Penelope's case first, we should start with members of the group that went to the meeting in the Cricketers. That was just before Penelope died, so it could easily be one of those that she annoyed," said Abigail. "Lillian, do you remember Verity Pikestaff from your days at the hospital?"

"I do. But I never spoke to her or anything. Nurses didn't have much to do with the funding for the hospital. She had an office on the fifth floor. I could go and watch her and see if any of the other Deads know anything."

"Great stuff. Betty and I can come with you. There's so many spirits there, and we might need to split up."

Betty said, "Ooh, yes, I'd like to follow her and do a bit of earwiggling. And at my age, there's always someone I know in one of the wards, so I'd love to go."

"Then Terry and Suzie, could you go to the Bonsons'? They've got the butchers in the high street, but he doesn't work there now he's got a string of shops. Does anyone know where they live?"

"I think they live out Pottlesham way. It's a big house called Virginia Lodge," said Betty. "I can't for the life of me think why he's even getting involved in the fun run. He's always been known for being an old skinflint."

"I heard tight as a duck's ar—"

"Ah, thank you, Terry," said Lillian, while looking at Suzie.

Betty added, "That's very true. Someone told me that he gets a sharp knife and cuts matchsticks down the middle to make two."

"Oh my God. I've just thought. I can remember his wife coming round years ago and apologising to me. Harvey had sent round his shirts and wanted me to unpick the collar on his old shirts and sew it back in the other way, to hide the worn-out bit. Same with the cuffs. As if he needed to do that."

"Apparently, Harvey said that Penelope would have the shirt off his back if he let her. I don't think anyone would want it. He's only helping out because his wife insisted he should. Their grandchild had been treated in the ward."

"So that just leaves Melody Myatt and the farmer, Sebastian March," said Abigail.

Hayley put up her finger. "Lady Caroline wants to help, so we could do both of those later today, if she's free. And she's met them, so that helps."

Suzie joined in. "I would love to go with Terry to the Bonsons'."

Abigail said, "Terry, make sure you get Suzie to check the drawers or files. See if you can see any bank statements. Perhaps they aren't as well off as they make out. He could have killed her to try and stop the run going ahead, so he didn't have to contribute."

Terry looked annoyed at the advice. "Don't tell your grandmother how to suck...what is it, Betty?"

"Terry! I don't think I should say in front of young company!"

Hayley shouted quickly, "It's eggs, Terry. Eggs! Can we change the subject, please? And Abigail was only trying to help." To which Terry apologised. The old Abigail would have given him a mouthful, but she remembered just in time that she had made a vow to be a bit nicer. But it sure was hard.

Suzie said, "We will, Abigail. There's nothing more I like than going through a suspect's house, but we'd have to do it today. Tomorrow we have to go back to the school in Chortle."

"Is everything alright with your brother, hun?"

"Yes, thanks, Hayley. Do you remember me telling you about the young girl that started in the first year, the same time as my best friend, Camille?"

"I do. It would have been you going to secondary school as well."

"Yes. We helped this Anya while we were there. She's like a lost soul. Just the sort that gets bullied. Even her teacher was making fun of her because she didn't like reading out loud, until we helped her. We think that she's being neglected or something. She says she lost her dad when she was younger, and they don't seem to have much of anything. I know poor doesn't mean she's not loved, but there is something not right."

"You do what you need to, hun. So shall we all do our visits today then? Hang on, I've got a phone call from Tom."

Hayley went into the corner, and no one could hear what was said. And they had all been trying.

"Bad news, I'm afraid. And I can't help feeling a bit responsible. I had the idea of leaving an anonymous message with the desk sergeant to say that I had seen someone running from Penelope's house after a scream. So Mills got a forensic team to check."

"That's marvellous, Hayley. So they're going to do something at last, are they?"

"Ah, that's the bad news. They've taken Lydia to Gorebridge Police Station for questioning!"

Lydia had answered the door and was surprised to see the two police constables who had come to her house when her mother had died. She invited them in, hoping to hear some good news, but couldn't believe it when they said Detective Chief Inspector Johnson wanted her to help them with their enquiries. Shouldn't they be helping her? She had a bad feeling as she grabbed her coat and bag and got in the police car.

"Arthur, Arthur. You'll never guess what. They've just arrested Lydia. Put her in a police car and carted her off. I'm going to ring Shirley. She'll be mad she didn't know first. Didn't I say, Arthur. ARTHUR!"

Sergeant Mills was sitting opposite Lydia Aston-Whyte in an informal room. There was no table separating them, for now.

"I'm very sorry for your loss, Lydia. And this is nothing to worry about. We just need a few details from you."

"You could have said that before. I'm still shaking."

"Please don't worry, miss. We want to give you an update on the case as well."

"So it is a case now?"

"Oh yes," said a scruffy man in a creased, grey suit and grey hair that was in urgent need of a barber. "You remember me, Miss Aston-Whyte? I'm going to call you Lydia. I don't hold with all those pretentious double-barrelled names."

"You're the one that made that joke about the cat."

"See, Sergeant, I said I'd be remembered for my jokes one day."

"I didn't say it was a good one."

"Nevertheless, you remembered it. Now let's get back to the case. We received an anonymous call yesterday, so you might be right about your mother's death. Someone heard feet running away after the scream. Two, not four," he said, waiting for a laugh that never came. "So, being a good detective…," which nearly got a laugh from Dave Mills, "I asked the sergeant here to get forensics to take a look. And they did find one anomaly. Near where the bottom of the ladder was, there were some begonias, which were pushed flat. They couldn't get a cast because there were so many flowers. I like begonias myself. The last wife always planted some as they lasted right into the autumn; nearly as long as our marriage. So that was very unlucky for the killer. So now we're thinking you were right. With the evidence of the neighbour, this other person, and an unknown footprint, there was someone else there."

"Good. So what are you going to do?"

"I'm glad you asked. We're going to check everyone's shoes to start with. Beginning with yours, of course."

"Why? I wasn't even there then."

Mills smiled at the petrified girl. "It's normal to check everyone's. We can eliminate you then."

Johnson ignored him. "Also, you might have run off and come back again. We've only got your word for it."

"What do you mean, come back? You sound like you think I did it."

"Do I? Maybe I do, or maybe I don't. But say I did, I'd want to know why you left work early, like you told the police on the day."

"My boss was off, and I'd had enough. I hate working there.

All I do is talk on the phone trying to sell people insurance they don't want."

"So, if I did, then there's a motive right there. Your mother was rich, wasn't she? Maybe I would think that she texted you to say she was going up the ladder when you were on your way, and you saw the opportunity."

"Do I need a solicitor, or a lawyer, whatever they are?"

"No, no," said Johnson with a sickly smile. "Just a few friendly questions, Lydia. I can't imagine a pretty little thing like you pushing over a heavy ladder. But who does get all her thousands and the big, detached house in the very desirable village of Becklesfield?" he said sarcastically.

"Actually, not that it's any of your business, my brother and I share her money. And she left the house to me."

"Well, isn't that nice? Do you hear that, Sergeant Mills? She gets the house. What a lucky girl."

Lydia's voice broke. "It doesn't have to be about money. Mummy made a lot of people angry when she kept asking for donations for her charity. I've watched them cross the road when they've seen her coming. And what about the ones at the meeting at the Cricketers before she fell? I heard there was nearly a fight between Mr Bonson and Sebastian March. He'd been knocking back the whiskies. And Verity Pikestaff from the hospital wasn't happy when Mum asked for printouts of other times she had given her money from CHAF. She wanted to know what the money had been spent on."

"CHAF?"

"Children's Hospital Appeal Fund."

"Chaf. You can get cream for that. Doesn't sound like something you'd want on a fun run, eh, Mills?"

"No, sir. Very droll."

"I hear you're doing the 10K, son. You and that useless Bennett. Hey, I've just thought, how did you know what was said at that meeting? And that there was nearly a fight. You said you didn't see her. You said you arrived just after the neighbour had found her."

Lydia went white and started to panic. How could she tell them that Hayley had got the information from her dead mum? How could she be so stupid? "Er, I can't remember now. You've got me all confused. Someone must have told me. Melody Myatt came round to pick up a folder; it must have been her."

"Have you seen any of the others that were there? Bearing in mind that we will be talking to them."

"I remember now, Mummy phoned me when she was walking home and told me. It was when I was still at work. With all that happened, I forgot. You can't be surprised. I saw my mum lying there dead," she sobbed.

"Good job her phone was in her pocket when she was taken to hospital then. I believe you saw it, Mills; did you see a phone call to Lydia that day?"

"No, sir, only texts." He felt so sorry for the young girl. He should have realised what Johnson would do and made sure her dad was there. But it wasn't like she was a minor. She was twenty-one. But he'd seen grown men in tears after being interrogated by his boss.

Johnson held out his hands. "But as I say, miss, it's just a friendly chat for now. So you sit here and make yourself comfortable, while me and Mills go and have a little discussion."

As soon as they had shut the door behind them, DCI Johnson rubbed his hands together and said, "Get all the evidence together, Sergeant. That young lady is as guilty as sin."

Chapter 10

HAYLEY WAS ON HER WAY TO PICK UP CAROLINE FROM Chiltern Hall. But first, she had made a stop outside Gorebridge General Hospital to drop off the others.

Abigail suddenly had doubts that she could do any good without Suzie. What could Betty or Lillian do either? How she wished she was alive again. There weren't many times when she felt that bad. She was dead, and she just had to get on with it. In some ways, it was better than being alive. But standing in the Accident and Emergency room, she felt so useless and helpless. She couldn't question Verity or any of her co-workers to see what she was like. She was the brains of the agency, but what good was that without a body? But she was just feeling sorry for herself.

She looked round to see where the other two were, but then she caught sight of Lillian. How could she be so selfish? Lillian was a nurse here in the children's ward until she had her life snatched away. She was even in her navy uniform.

"Are you okay, Lillian?"

"I miss the life. I was good at my job. See that lady over there? She's struggling to breathe, and I can't do anything. And that little girl has a fever. She could convulse any minute, and there's nothing I can do to help her. That young nurse hasn't even noticed. And see that old man on the trolley? A young boy is standing next to him, so he must be near to dying. I'm a nurse, but what good would I be now?"

"There's always something we can do, Lillian," said Betty, as she went over to the boy and asked him, "Is this your grandfather, dear?"

"No, it's my father. He's had a long wait to see me. He's thought of me every day since I died. So I made sure I was here."

"How old were you?"

"I was thirteen. I climbed a tree in the woods. He told me not to, but I didn't listen. I never did. I've come back to take him home. He's looked forward to this day all his life. He never doubted he would see me again."

"I don't think either of you have long to wait. This is Lillian; she was a nurse here once. What's your name?"

"William Foster."

"Hello, William. I've had a look at your father, and I can tell from his colour and his breathing that he will soon pass, so don't worry. He won't wake up again or feel any pain at all. Watch his chest; any minute now it will rise and fall for the last time. Take his hand."

"Pop, I'm here. You can rest now. I've got you."

The old man felt his hand move and opened his eyes. "Well, I never, William. Is it really you?"

"It sure is, Pop. Mum's waiting. Come on, it's time." The three spirits watched as the old man and his son walked away. The young nurse went to find a doctor to come and have a look at Mr Foster. Something was wrong.

"Thanks for that, Betty," said Lillian.

"Just remember, you look after Suzie now, like you promised

her mother. And all of us. Where would we be without our own nurse?"

Abigail added gently, "She's right. And when we have a murder, you can tell us how they died and when. We'd be lost without you. And what we do is important. We need to remind ourselves of that sometimes. When I think of all the people we've put away and even the lives we've saved, we should be very proud of what we've achieved. And we will get justice for Penelope too. And we'll find out what happened to poor Bones. So come on, chin up, tell us where we're likely to find Verity Pikestaff."

"She used to have an office on the fifth floor. That's where all the administrators are. She might still be there. Come on, I'll show you."

Abigail wasn't too keen on going up in the lift after the one in the hotel, so they walked up the stairs.

"Now this is the best thing about being dead, girls," said Betty. "Before I died, I'd have needed oxygen and a Sherpa to get me up here. But now I'm as fit as a schoolgirl, if I wasn't dead."

"I reckon we'll have no trouble doing that fun run. We'll be at the finish line before they've all made it to the top," said Abigail. "Hayley won't know what's hit her. Actually, I've never been so fit since I've been dead. See, Lillian, there's always a bright side."

Verity Pikestaff's name was on the same door, and they went in. She wasn't there, but there was a lot of paperwork spread over her desk that they hoped would give them some clues.

"No photos of a partner or kids," said Betty. "I wish Suzie was here to go through her drawers."

"Yes, we need to find out if anyone else was," joked Abigail. "What did she look like, Lillian?"

"Very attractive, but not pretty. Kind of hard-looking. Brown hair, perfect teeth. She always wore bright red lipstick."

"Well, that's a sure sign," said Betty. "'Red lips sink ships.' They said that in the war."

"Loose," Lillian corrected.

"Definitely," said Betty seriously. "Ada Grimshaw was. Even my John, who, as you know, liked…"

"We better keep going in case she gets back. Not that it matters," said Abigail. "No calendar; that's a shame. A diary, but that only shows today. Er, ring James—could be a boyfriend. Two o'clock, meeting with Gordon. That's in a couple of hours. Then eight o'clock tonight, the Greyhound Pub."

"Why don't you and Terry go on one of your dates," suggested Betty.

"As long as no one is murdered." Abigail frowned as she thought of the times that they had gone somewhere for a romantic time only to have something gruesome happen. Oh, who was she kidding, she loved it. "I suppose for the sake of the investigation, I could go. I wonder who she's meeting there. Now this is interesting," said Abigail as she looked under the desk. "Here's her handbag. The door must be locked with this left here. Because this bag is a designer one; an Andre Duvall. Worth about six hundred pounds."

"How do you know?" asked Lillian.

"I might not have been rich myself, but most of my customers were. Sometimes I'd take a pair of scissors to clothes worth hundreds. It could be a bit worrying, I tell you. But one of them had this exact bag, and she told me all about it. Hers was in blue and gold, but this is it, I'm sure. See, there's the logo."

"She might have a good job here, but no way would the NHS pay her that much. Unless she got paid an awful lot more than I did as a nurse."

"That wouldn't surprise me. Hang on, I can hear something." They all heard voices and the jangling of keys. A woman with brown hair, looking to be in her thirties, entered with a grey-haired man who had a stethoscope around his neck.

"I've already told you, Giles, it's nothing to do with me. If I had the resources, you could have your machine. The budget is used up for this year. It's not up to me."

"This isn't the end of this, Verity," he shouted, as he stormed out and marched up the corridor.

Verity slammed the door after him and sat down behind her desk. She reached down and picked up her expensive handbag and rifled through it. The ghosts all peered in but couldn't see anything. Lillian saw a red purse, but that was it. Verity found what she was looking for and leant back in her chair.

"An electronic cigarette. I was not expecting that," said Abigail.

"She could get fired for smoking that in here. But if she's been cooking the books, that's no worry for her. She hasn't even bothered opening the window. She's a cool one, that's for sure," said Lillian.

"More than capable of pushing over a ladder," agreed Betty.

There were footsteps outside, and Verity quickly pulled open the top drawer and dropped the e-cigarette in.

"Knock knock, gorgeous."

"Ryan, I told you not to just burst in. I could have been with someone."

"No, you couldn't. You know you've only got eyes for me."

Abigail asked Lillian, "Do you recognise him?"

"Don't think so. He might be new. But he doesn't look like a doctor or a nurse. Maybe management."

"So, gorgeous, where are we going tonight? Your place?"

"Well, it can't be yours, can it? Unless you've told your wife about us."

"No, but I will. I said I would, didn't I?" he said, as he kissed the back of her neck.

She shrugged him off. "Not here, I told you."

"So where tonight? Shall I meet you at the restaurant?"

"I can't tonight. My mother is in town, and she's coming

over. I'm making her lasagne and my famous Pavlova. But I promise I'll see you tomorrow night and give you a treat. And I don't mean my Pavlova."

"Okay then. Don't forget that other business. I'm going to need those figures."

Abigail said thoughtfully, "So she's a liar, seeing a married man, and there's someone else that wants to see her figures. And he's already seen her figure by the sound of it. She's gone straight to the top of my list. So I wonder who she's meeting at the Greyhound tonight."

Betty said, "Whoever it is, I bet the dollar on my bottom that it's another man."

"Me too, Betty. Me too."

Chapter 11

HAYLEY HAD PICKED UP LADY CAROLINE HATTON, AND together they called on the unsuspecting Melody Myatt. They were using the excuse that Hayley wanted to help, and they asked her if there was anything she needed. The two visitors saw straight away from her puffy, bloodshot eyes that Melody had been crying more than once.

Hayley felt she had to ask, "I'm sorry, have we come at a bad time? We can come back later."

Melody sniffed and wiped her eyes with a tissue. "No. Come in. I think it just hit me today that Penny has really gone."

"Were you close?"

"We'd worked together for years. I will miss her. She could be rather domineering and forceful, but that was just her. Underneath it, she was very kind and always wanted to help others."

Hayley nodded. "I know someone like that. She's very bossy, but sometimes we need someone like that in our lives. To keep things moving. And if anyone hurts any of her friends, she'll move Heaven and earth to help them."

"That's exactly right. Penny was just like that. I don't know how anything is going to carry on now. I might have to cancel the run. But then the children wouldn't get their money."

Lady Caroline said softly, "There are plenty of people that can help. I intend to, and I run committees that would only be too pleased to get involved. I don't think you could cancel now anyway. It's a week on Saturday, and you've sold so many tickets that you'd never be able to give all the money back. Then there's the food that would go to waste, and the bands would have to be cancelled. I don't even know who the stars of the show are."

"Penny made me swear on her life that I wouldn't tell. Oh no, that sounds awful. And I promise I didn't and still won't. I've got all the details."

"You can do it. Please reconsider, Melody."

"If you think we can. I know wherever Penny is, she would want the show to go on. Do you think she is looking down on us?"

Hayley smiled and said, "I can assure you that she is. It's almost like she's still here."

"Did you mean it, Caroline, when you said the police thought it might not be an accident?"

"I think they're certain now. Have you any idea who would have wanted her dead?"

"Of course not. She was the loveliest lady I've ever known. I don't know if I can carry on without her. I mean for the charity, of course."

"You'll be fine. You're stronger than you think you are," said Hayley. But she couldn't help but wonder if Melody's feelings for her friend were a little more than a colleague would feel.

"Is there anyone we can call for you? Have you got any family?"

"No, I never married. Never found the right person. Don't worry about me." Melody sat up straight. "I've just got to get on with life. Penny would say, 'Pull yourself together, woman'.

Thank you for your offer of help, but if you wouldn't mind, I'd like to be on my own now."

Hayley and Caroline got in Hayley's car, and they both felt sorry for her.

"I think she truly loved her, Caroline. I felt it in my heart."

"I think so too. So are you saying that she would never hurt her?"

"No. I think I'm saying a woman scorned is capable of doing anything. Including pushing an unrequited lover off a ladder! But I really hope she isn't guilty."

"Me too. I doubt Penelope had any idea how she actually felt. But then again, maybe she had told her and didn't get the response that she wanted. We can't exclude her yet. So where now, Hayley?"

"I think straight to Polehanger Farm. It's where the race starts, so it will be interesting to see how things are going, and then have a chat with Sebastian March."

"Good idea. Do you know anything about him?"

"Sebastian March? I tried to, but no one seems to know him. I did ask around. Tom said he bought the place about two years ago. I've no idea if it has animals or grows wheat or something. I should know all about it because my nan and grandad had a farm. But when you're young, you don't take much notice of how a farm works. I know grandad used to have to get up at five every day for first milk. That's about it."

"Must have been lovely visiting as a child."

"It was. I used to have a little Shetland pony called Racer, I just remembered. And I stayed with them during the summer holidays. It was a happy childhood. I hope I'll be able to give my child the same. I sometimes worry with what I do."

"You'll be a lovely, kind mum. There's no doubt about that. Are you thinking of having children?"

"Tom wants to. Actually, so do I, but I'm in no hurry. I want to give my baby everything that I had. Trips to a fair, or the seaside. They were the happiest days of my life. Do you want children, hun?"

"I'd better get married first. But I'd love a family. And I don't want my cousin taking over Chiltern Hall either. So I've definitely got to have an heir. But we've both got plenty of time."

"That's true. It can take a while. We have been trying, but with Tom's job he can either be home too late or be too tired. But we'll get there in the end. I've even bought some wool so I can knit some bits. Can you knit? Could you teach me?"

"Good God, no. I think my nanny that used to look after me tried to teach me once. I nearly had her eye out, so she didn't bother again. It's really hard. You have to do every single stitch! I cast on twenty stitches, but by the time I had done a couple of inches, I had about thirty for some reason. So I could show you, but a baby cardigan might fit a ten-year-old by the time you've finished."

"It will probably take me ten years to make anyway, so that might be handy. Perhaps I'll have to ask Betty then. Right, let's go and see Old MacDonald."

"Oh, he's not old. Early thirties, I'd say. And rather nice."

"I say, Caroline, you like him."

Caroline blushed. "Maybe I do. You wait till you see him. I used to go to a lot of Young Farmers events when I was younger, but there wasn't one as gorgeous as him."

"Well, you wanted to get married. I better start looking at hats."

"A bit early, darling. But you never know. Landowners and the gentry have been pairing off for centuries, so why not? But he did give me the collywobbles when I first saw him."

"Well, that's a word you don't hear every day. Must be love."

"Wait till you see him. He is rather gorgeous."

Hayley thought Caroline was right. She would even go so far as to say drop-dead gorgeous. Sebastian March had seen a small, red Mini coming down the short drive and went out to meet them. He was dressed as Hayley had imagined he would be. Grey corduroy trousers, plaid shirt and a tight, grey waistcoat. He looked every inch the affluent farmer. He flicked his coiffured fringe out of his eyes and held his hand out to Caroline.

"Lady Caroline, how lovely to see you again. Is there anything wrong? I wasn't expecting a visit."

"No, nothing wrong, Sebastian. I said I would help Melody and just wanted to see if you needed anything. This is my friend, Hayley Bennett. She'll be running with me, and also helping out with the arrangements."

He shook hands with Hayley and invited them into the farmhouse.

"How old is the building?" asked Hayley as they went into the small hall.

"Only about one hundred and fifty years. Which is quite new I'm told around these parts. I'm sure Chiltern Hall is much older."

"Parts of it go back centuries. I'll have to give you the guided tour one day," answered Caroline.

Sebastian gave her a smile that gave her the collywobbles again. Hayley felt a bit of a gooseberry as he said, "I'd like that very much. Perhaps I could thank you by taking you to dinner afterwards."

"Yes, I'd like that very much. But we better get on. We've got an awful lot to do."

"I'm sorry, come in. Shall we go in the kitchen? I always think it's the heart of a farmhouse."

Hayley said, "Oh, yes. My grandparents had a farm, and we spent most of the time in the kitchen, sitting around the table. Pine, very much like this one. Even the Welsh dresser takes me back. You're probably like Grandad, always in and out with dirty boots, so it makes sense." Hayley looked towards the door, but she couldn't see any sign of muddy wellingtons. Maybe he left them outside.

"I know what you mean, my family has farmed for generations. I've got a foreman, who does most of the day-to-day work, and he lives in the village, so I never get my hands, or my boots, too dirty. Let's have a coffee before we get down to business."

"Thank you, Sebastian, that would be lovely," said Caroline. "Which field are the tents going to be in?"

"The one on the right as you came up the drive. At the far end is where the stage is going to be for the bands. I don't suppose you know who the surprise guests are, do you? Penelope wouldn't say in case it became about them and not the charity."

"Penelope swore Melody to silence, so not a clue, I'm afraid. There's a couple of local bands, and then they'll go on. I've no idea if they're arriving by helicopter. We literally know nothing at all."

"Oh well, it'll be a nice surprise on the night. I just hope it isn't going to rain. It won't do the instruments much good."

"It won't do my new tent much good," blurted out Hayley, without thinking.

"Are you staying, Caroline? I can't imagine you in a tent though."

Caroline was slightly annoyed at the comment. "Why ever not? I'm as hardy as the next person. I backpacked all around Scotland in a two-man tent. And we had midges the size of bumblebees."

Sebastian held up his hands. "I'm sorry," he laughed. "I stand corrected."

"But no," she smiled. "It put me off for life. It was cold, uncomfortable, and I swore I would never do it again."

"I have two spare rooms, so I would be honoured if you wanted to stay here."

"I was going to get the chauffeur to pick me up, but I will think about it," she said coyly. Hayley was beginning to think she was invisible. But how perfect would they look together, she thought. And the babies would be adorable. But she was getting even more carried away. But there was definitely chemistry between them.

Hayley wanted to get the topic round to Penelope. "Did you hear that the police now think that Penelope was definitely murdered?"

"You're joking. I thought she just fell off a ladder. Why would they think it was murder?"

"Forensics, apparently. Whatever that means. And her daughter says she was used to going up and down one. They have no idea who it is yet. What about you?"

"I can assure you it wasn't me," he said with a smile.

"No. I mean do you have any idea who it could have been?"

"She was a very forceful lady, and I'm sure that would have annoyed a lot of people, but not really. Harvey Bonson told me he couldn't stand the woman. But I can't see him going that far. And I get the feeling he didn't like any woman much. I expect it was one of her family. It usually is someone they know in these cases. The husband mainly, I think. I know very little about her, so I don't know if she was even married or had children. No doubt the police will look into that."

Lady Caroline said, "She was divorced and he had remarried, but they'll be checking all her family and friends. Including you, I'm afraid, Sebastian."

"All sounds rather exciting. I've never been questioned by the police before. Not that there's much I can tell them. I had left my car in the pub's car park and drove straight home. I did see her walking off down the road towards her house. I wish I had offered her a lift now. But between you and me, I wanted to get home as quickly as I could. I was probably over the limit to drive, strictly speaking. Not by much, but probably in a court of law."

"Maybe not mention that to the police," said Caroline.

The three of them discussed more about the details of the

fun run and where things were going to be on the farm, and then Sebastian walked them back to the car.

Hayley asked, "How many acres have you got here?"

"About two hundred. We have a dairy herd, but mainly we grow wheat and barley. The harvest was abundant this year. We had plenty of sun and just enough rain."

"I expect you have to rest the fields. What was it that Grandad called it? Er, tallow, I think. Is that right?"

"Yes, we tallow the fields. Well, don't forget your offer of a guided tour. I'll hold you to it, you know, Lady Caroline."

"It's a date. Bye, Sebastian." Hayley might just as well have not been there.

"That went well," said a grinning Caroline as they drove away.

"You little minx. You were actually flirting, the pair of you."

"What on earth do you mean?"

"You know. 'I'd love to give you a tour of the Hall, Sebastian'. I bet you will," laughed Hayley.

"Don't you think he's total perfection?"

"Drop-dead, yeah. But there is one thing that worries me. He's no farmer. Even I know you fallow a field. You don't tallow it! And there were a few things that were missing."

"Like what?"

"There were no tractors or farm machinery, no muddy boots, and the strangest of all, no dog."

Chapter 12

TERRY AND SUZIE WALKED UP POTTLESHAM HIGH Street and were nearly out the other side of the village before they saw the entrance to Virginia Lodge. Even that was nearly hidden by huge, overgrown laurel bushes that lined the driveway. As soon as they turned in, they saw why it was so called. The entire front of the large, dark-bricked house was covered in Virginia creeper. It gave it an eerie look—creepy, thought Terry. The leaves were already turning to a vibrant red, as autumn was approaching fast.

There were no cars parked outside, and the garage door was open, so they could only assume that no one was home.

"There must be a lot of money in meat," said Suzie, as they took in the size of the grand house.

"They've got about eight shops down here. They weren't around when I was alive. It was Beckett & Sons in Becklesfield then. And he was never that well-off. He only had a flat above the shop for himself and the kids."

"Shame neither of them are home. We can't get much if we don't even see what they're like."

"You can tell a lot about a man by how he lives. Come on, Suzie, let's go in and do a search."

Although they didn't need to, they entered through the heavy oak door. Terry couldn't feel it, but Suzie felt a chill in the air.

"Oh, Terry, it's freezing in here. Usually it's us that make the room temperature drop."

"The walls are thick, and there's a lot of overhanging trees, but I think it's what Betty was saying. Bonson is as mean as muck. No heating, I reckon."

"Oh yes. Tight old man. His poor wife. Even the furniture looks old."

"And there's not much of it. The rumours I heard must be true. The carpet looks like it's seen better days."

They walked into the living room, where two huge sofas filled the room. They were upholstered in brown with orange flowers—a colour scheme that included the curtains.

Terry said, "Good God. I'm sure these were all the rage when I was alive. That cupboard and table look old. Not antique-old, just old. I had that half-table with the green pretend-leather on the top. Hey, they've even got a lava lamp."

"What's a lava lamp?"

"It's that thing here. The oil heats up and blobs go up and down. You weren't anyone until you had a lava lamp. Or a china horse and cart like that one."

Suzie pulled a face. "Really? I can't quite see why they were popular. I suppose Mum liked her candles. Tastes change. I'm enjoying doing this with you, Terry. Do you remember when we were looking for where your parents were buried?"

"Remember? I'll always be grateful to you. I wouldn't have found the old wooden crosses if you hadn't moved the leaves and the moss away. It's a very special talent you have."

"Is it because I'm a child, do you think?"

"I'm not sure. But I know a lot of the youngsters do have the ability. Do you think this is their daughter?" Terry pointed to a young, dark-haired girl in various stages of her life, from a toddler to a teen. The others were of a young boy, and on the sideboard was a photograph of a wedding, with him as the groom and the Bonsons on either side of the young couple. Terry thought the butcher was a lot thinner in those days. Mrs Bonson was a tall, well-built lady with a beaming smile under a large-brimmed hat as mother-of-the-groom.

"What are we looking for, do you think, Terry?"

"I don't know till I see it. There's not much here. Can you open the drawer on the sideboard? Remember what Abigail said."

"Of course. Mmm, here's a bank statement. Gosh. Why is he so mean when he's got so much money?"

"That's why he's got so much. The rich don't like spending. Well, he doesn't. Is that a tax bill?"

"There's a lot of bills. Some are in red. What does that mean?"

"It means he's late paying them. Doesn't want to part with his money until the last minute, would be my guess."

"Here's some receipts. Raynes Dresses of London for Sally Bonson. Blimey, three thousand pounds. A spa weekend at the Courtridge Hotel. I wish my mum could do that. She deserves it after what she's been through. More receipts for hairdressers, a necklace, and other things for Mrs Bonson. He doesn't keep her short."

"That doesn't match his personality at all."

"Maybe it's love. But looking at the photos of them, they look like the least likely lovebirds that I've seen."

"Perhaps she had more right to the money. They came from up north. Either she worked with him from the start, or maybe she put up the money. But we're here to see if Harvey wanted to kill Penelope. There hasn't been anything so far."

"What would Abigail say?" Suzie counted off the motives on

her fingers. "She saw him doing something he shouldn't have been."

"Yes. If his wife held the purse strings and Penelope told her about an affair or something dodgy, then he might be out on his ear."

"Two. He was in love with her. Or she was in love with him. No, I can't see that. Three. She had something to blackmail him over."

"Like he was selling donkey or horse meat instead of beef."

Suzie was horrified. "Oh, he wouldn't do that, would he?"

"It has been known. But no. I've only heard how good his meat is. Mind you, he might be chopping up dead bodies and putting them in his sausages."

"Yuk. If I'm reincarnated, remind me to be a vegetarian."

"They were both well known in the community, so their paths could have crossed somewhere. Penelope had a lot of fingers in a lot of pies."

"Maybe one of them was donkey," laughed Suzie. "One of them liked whisky by the looks of it. There's more bottles in here than in a shop."

"He looks like a whisky-man. Red face and everything. Let's see what you can find in here. God, even the kitchen looks like something out of the eighties. They've even still got one of those auto-chop things. That's probably an antique now. I got one and I think I only used it a few times, and then realised it took more time to wash it up than would ever take to get out a knife. It doesn't look like they do a lot of cooking, though. Can you open the fridge, please, Suzie?"

"There's a lot of meat. Steaks, aren't they? And wine. They both liked a drink then."

"Abigail won't be pleased if we don't find out a bit more. Let's go upstairs. We'll be able to find out if they share the same room. That can be a sign of a happy marriage or not. Mind you, going by the size of him, it might be because he snores."

"Or maybe she does. Abigail says we should never just assume these things."

"And she's right. She usually is," Terry said with a sigh. "Yep. Separate rooms, I thought it would be. He sleeps in here and watches the television before he goes to sleep. And smokes a cigar," as he pointed to a dirty ashtray by his bed. "There used to be an ashtray when I was young. It was a bit like the lava lamp; they all had them. It was shaped like a skull and said on it, 'Poor old Fred, smoked in bed'. That would be worth something as well."

Suzie opened his wardrobe, which was falling apart. "Just old-fashioned dad trousers and jackets. White shirts and some ties. He didn't spend money on his clothes like she did. There's nothing personal here." On the top of his tall-boy, as Terry called it, was a brass tray for putting his change on that contained mostly pennies. And a pair of cufflinks with a symbol on that Terry had seen before. He wondered if Harvey Bonson was a Freemason. Could that be important? He would tell Abigail. No doubt she'd know all about that.

"Let's try Mrs Bonson's room, Suzie."

"Definitely more of a woman's room." The curtains were pink and frilly, and the dressing table had china ornaments and a white orchid. Next to her bed, there was a photograph of the same young girl that was downstairs.

"I reckon that's her granddaughter, Terry. She's pretty, isn't she? Takes after her mum. Look, a china doll. Why do they always look so scary? Like they're going to suddenly move when you're not looking."

"That one looks very creepy. That is an antique, I'd say. Victorian."

Suzie picked up a book that was face down on her dressing table. *Love is Forever*.

"Another surprise. I thought she'd be a thriller person. You can't tell a book by its cover, and you can't tell a book reader by what they read. Doesn't mean she wouldn't be capable of killing a rival. Anyone that can skin a rabbit and put it in a pot could push a ladder over, Suzie."

"Rabbit? Yuk. That's disgusting."

"We often ate rabbit in the home when I was young. Cheap meat and plenty of it. Not so much now. I can't remember the last time I saw a rabbit hopping around in the village."

"Bonsons have cooked them all. I hope he killed her and they lock him up. Poor little bunnies."

Terry thought he had better change the subject before she found out what venison was. "Here's a bottle of sleeping pills. Probably so she can't hear him snoring. But I just can't see him following Penelope home and killing her. He drives an old Rolls Royce, and I'm sure someone would have noticed that anywhere near Bellringers Close."

"Now the police are involved, they can check their alibis. Something happened in that meeting, Terry. I feel it in my bones."

"I do. Let's get back to Becklesfield. Maybe the others have had more luck. We'll all say what we've learned, and then Abigail can sort out what's important. She's good at that, but don't tell her I said so. She's bigheaded enough as it is!"

Chapter 13

BACK IN BECKLESFIELD, THE OTHERS HAD ALL MET AT Hayley's house in Church Lane. Lady Caroline had to go to a meeting of the Pottery Society, and Tom was still at work in Gorebridge. They waited until Terry and Suzie got back from the Bonsons', and then they all retailed what they had learned about the suspects.

"I think it might be Melody, unfortunately," said Hayley. "Unrequited love. Although that Sebastian is no farmer."

"No, it's Verity Pikestaff. Never trust a floozie, my old mum used to say," said Betty.

Suzie added, "That Harvey Bonson seems a horrible man. I reckon it's him."

"In other words," said Abigail, "we don't have a clue. They've all got reasons, but none that really stand out. I'm thinking more of Verity, as it looks like she's been taking money from the fundraising. Perhaps Terry and I will find something out at the pub tonight."

"Maybe it was a drug deal gone wrong," said Betty excitedly. She always put forward that scenario, but she hadn't been right yet. "I wonder who she's meeting. I'd love to come." She saw the look on Terry's face and said, "But I won't, dear. I wouldn't want to be a raspberry. You two enjoy yourselves."

"We will, Betty. It's our fourth date, isn't it, love?"

"Must be by now. That would nearly have been a record when I was alive," joked Abigail.

So that evening, Terry and Abigail held hands and walked through the village to the Greyhound Pub, which was on the road that led to Chiltern Hall. They arrived about ten minutes before Verity Pikestaff was due. Only half the tables were taken, so they took the one near the bar, which had a good view of the entrance.

"I'll have a pint, please, barman."

"I'll have a large white wine. Shame we're dead, isn't it?"

"I miss a pint more than anything."

"I could eat the world's biggest box of chocolates. I'd even eat the fudge ones. They say life's not fair, but death is even worse. Imagine if we got to Heaven and we could have all the chocolate and beer we wanted. And I didn't get fat, and you never fell over or had a hangover."

"Quick, where's that light?"

"Seriously though, do you think you'll ever move on, Terry? I mean to the other, other side."

"Maybe. But not when there's a beautiful blonde to keep me here. She's very special. And clever and kind."

"I think I know her. She's perfect."

"She is for me. I wish we didn't have to look out for that Verity. She couldn't hold a candle to you. Let's not bother. I want to carry on like this, looking into your beautiful, blue eyes." He picked up her hand.

"Oh, Terry, you're so special to me. I don't think I've ever…"

Terry sat up. "Wow. Who's that? What a cracker," as a beautiful lady wearing red lipstick walked in.

Abigail snatched her hand back. "Well, thank you. That's the one you didn't want to look for, Verity Pikestaff."

"Really? She's not a patch on you, though, love. I thought it was her; that's why I pointed her out."

"Yeah. A likely story. Sorry, too little, too late, Terry Styles. You're dead to me."

"Very funny."

"And I was trying to change and be nice."

"Really? I hadn't noticed."

"Well, thank you. Look, let's just do what we came for, keep an eye on her, and see who she meets."

"Oh well, if I must," said Terry.

The trouble was that all the men looked at her as she walked in. Verity went to the bar to order a drink as the door opened again.

"Well, well, well. I don't believe it," said Terry. A large man with a florid face joined her. "That is Harvey Bonson, the butcher. That's opened up more possibilities."

"Surely they're not a couple. I'd have seen everything then. Maybe we could make it if they can. If I ever forgive you, that is. I'll have you know I used to turn heads when I went in a pub. Or was it stomachs? Can't remember now."

"See, that's why I love you. You make me laugh."

"And you've never seen me with all my make-up on. I would have to die without it."

"You don't need it. You're a natural beauty. Yes, she's pretty, sexy, classy…"

"You can stop if you like. You're really not helping."

"But it's all on the surface. Take off the make-up and the lipstick, and you wouldn't recognise her. I only want you. Cross my heart and hope to die in a cellar full of rats."

"Mmm. That doesn't mean an awful lot under the circumstances, but I forgive you. Come on, they're going to that table. Let's join them."

Harvey Bonson and Verity Pikestaff had taken a table for four, and Terry and Abigail sat on the spare chairs to listen in.

"How are you doing, Harvey?"

"Me? I'm fine, lassie. Sally isn't too good at the minute. I know it's been a long time, but it doesn't get any easier, does it?"

"I know. Does she feel better now that she's doing something to help the hospital?"

"She's not doing much. But it does help. It's mostly me doing all the donating and the hard work. She doesn't know about the other business. I can't tell her that. I'd do anything for her, but I can't tell her. I have to protect her."

"I nearly didn't tell you, but you've got the right to know, same as me. Is everything in place? He'll be there, I take it?"

"Yes, as far as I know. This business with Penelope nearly cocked it right up. Do you think there's any connection?"

"I can't work it out, Harvey. How could she know? I was wondering if it was you because she found out. Sorry, I'm sure it was just an accident. We've just got to forget about her. I can't say I liked the woman anyway. She had it in for me, as you know."

"I wondered if it was you who pushed the woman off the ladder. But you're right, let's forget about her. We've got enough to do."

"I'm terrified and excited at the same time, Harvey. I don't even care if we're caught. It has to be done, for them."

He raised a glass. "To the fun run. And to Louise and Cheryl."

Terry and Abigail looked at each other, and she said, "Who the hell are Louise and Cheryl? And whatever they are going to do, it's happening at the fun run. But don't worry, I know exactly who can help. I'll get Hayley to take me to see Celia at the paper as soon as she can."

Hayley and Caroline dropped off Abigail and Betty at the offices of the *Chiltern Weekly* in Gorebridge to see Celia Hanson. They had decided to have one last day at the gym and were hoping they could bump into Maria Dubois, the owner.

Terry had met a new Dead near the church and volunteered to show him the ropes. Which was ironic as the gentleman had been a naval officer in life. Lillian and Suzie had gone across the fields to check up on her old friend, Camille, and the very vulnerable Anya.

Abigail knew that Celia spent all her time in the news offices, where she had been one of their top journalists when she was alive. Most of her articles were to do with inquests and what happened in court cases. Abigail was able to help her, and now she often helped with the cases of the agency. Her knowledge saved a lot of trawling through papers in the library, as she had an eidetic memory and could recall anything that was written about or had been said.

The only thing Abigail was never too pleased about was the fact that Celia was immaculately dressed in a business suit, without a hair out of place when she died, unlike Abigail herself. She, unfortunately, had died in bed, complete with bed hair at the back.

They found her in the editor's office, looking over his shoulder unseen, at what was going into the paper that week.

"Hello, you two. What can I do for you? Is it about the murder of Penelope Aston-Whyte? I hate to tell you, but I don't know a thing. Shall we go and talk somewhere more comfortable?"

They found a table in the reception area, and Abigail told Celia what they needed.

"It is connected to Penelope's death in a way. There's something odd going on with a couple of people she knew. You might know them; Harvey Bonson and Verity Pikestaff."

"I know him. He owns Bonson's Butchers."

Betty said, "She works at the hospital in administration and wears red lipstick!"

"Oh well, she's obviously guilty. What exactly do you want from me?"

Abigail explained. "We heard them talking and two names came up. Louise and Cheryl. I'm thinking Louise Pikestaff or Bonson, or Cheryl Pikestaff or Bonson."

Celia looked up at the ceiling, using her photographic memory and deep in thought. "Hmm. Louise Pikestaff - aged seventeen. Died June 2012. Suspected drug overdose. Cheryl Bonson - aged fifteen. Took a contaminated ecstasy pill. Died in Gorebridge Hospital in July 2012."

"Oh, my giddy aunt," said Betty. "I was right at last. It was a drug deal gone wrong. And that's why there were only photos of the girl up to when she was a teenager in Harvey's house. How sad."

"Drugs? Well done, Betty. Was anyone arrested in connection with the deaths?"

"Not arrested, no. Let me think. There were two suspects. One was Frank, or rather Francis Walker, a local thug, but he had an alibi. Then there was Louise's boyfriend. He was presumed guilty, because he disappeared completely. His name was, er, Elliot Thornton. As far as I know, he was never found or caught."

Abigail went quiet and frowned while deep in thought. "Now this is a bit of a leap, Celia, but have you got a description of this Elliot? His age and anything else?"

"Brown hair, about eighteen. Dressed in jeans and a black hoodie with an eagle on it."

"Bones!" Abigail and Betty shouted together.

"Bones?"

"Hayley met a lovely boy who had been buried in the grounds of Chartridge Castle about twelve years ago, so 2012. It's a hotel and spa now. He can't remember a thing about who killed him, and I promised I would help. At least we have a name now. I don't suppose you know if he has a family we could contact, do you?"

"Naturally. He had a mother and older brother. She lived locally. I didn't know where. Of course, she may have moved."

"Celia, you're marvellous. But I'm not sure it helps us with Penelope. I can't see her as a drug dealer. There must be another reason she had to die. Perhaps she found out that they were going to take revenge on someone at the fun run. That could be anyone that's going. Man or woman. It sounded like they had only just found out who was responsible for their deaths. And that person was going to be there as well. Hayley said Sebastian didn't seem much of a farmer, so we need Tom to do a check on him. It will have to be after the campathon, though. Let's hope it's not too late. And what was Melody Myatt doing twelve years ago? And Verity worked at a hospital; that could even be important. Perhaps she supplied the drugs. We need to find out."

Betty said, "What about the band that's booked for that night? It could be one of them. Bands and drugs can go together. Maybe Harvey and Verity are going to kill two stones with one bush. Nobody knows who the big name is. Maybe someone blamed Penelope for booking them."

"That's very true. We'll know it all on Saturday. You've helped us so much again, Celia. I don't think much can be found out before then. We'll just have to be there and hope we can stop something happening at the fun run. If not another murder!"

Chapter 14

A DESOLATE MAN SAT ON HIS BED. HIS GAUNT FACE and loose collar laid testament to this. He was so lonely, despite being surrounded by people. Most of them he was too frightened to talk to, and the others, he daren't mix with. He was just one of a vast population of thieves, thugs and murderers. But he wasn't any of those things. He had tried all his life to be good and do the right thing. He went to church when he was growing up, and had never even had a parking ticket. Until that night.

He was lying two feet away from a man who had killed someone with a single punch—just because he didn't like the way he drove. He had to make sure he didn't say anything the man wouldn't like, and tried his best to agree with everything he said.

In his prison cell, he started to shake from his head down as he heard a fight going on somewhere. He hadn't really stopped shaking since he'd been sentenced. Innocent or guilty, you were treated the same, he'd been told. He'd been found guilty, so it was tough. Half of them said they were innocent, so he was stuck there for the rest of his life. He picked up her last letter. She still loved him. She would wait for him. She knew he didn't do it. She was finding it hard, though; he could tell by her writing. He put his hand under his pillow and found her first letter. He had to hide them from his cellmate. It was the only thing he had that was his own. That first letter was full of hope, saying he'd be out soon and not to give up. But her childlike writing, which she still had at the age of forty, was now a wispy scrawl, and she didn't sound so sure he would ever be home again.

She had stopped coming to see him a few months ago. It had been his idea. It was no place for a gentle soul like her. It was too hard to see her go, anyway.

He had to try and get help from somewhere. But there was no one who could help. His appeal had failed. He would have said a prayer, but that hadn't worked in the past, so he didn't bother. Maybe he would die. And he prayed for that instead. There had been three suicides in his wing of the Category B prison already. That was another option that gave him hope. Or maybe he could starve to death. The food was inedible, and he didn't know how he was surviving on the food that he did eat. He dreaded to think what had been put in it, after all; they thought he was a murderer.

He knew he was one of the lucky ones; his cell had a window. Not big, but just enough to see the sky and sometimes the moon. The same moon that his wife was under. The lights went out, and he put the letters as quietly as he could under his pillow. He hoped to dream of being somewhere with his family, but he didn't always. Most of the time, he dreamed that he was locked in a house, with hideous monsters trying to get to him. Then he would wake in a cold sweat and realise he was. The man made up a story in his head where the guilty person would come forward, and he would be freed. But he knew he didn't have a chance in hell.

Chapter 15

Hayley was hoping to not be quite so hot and sweaty when she met Maria Dubois, but that was exactly how she looked as they went into the bar after their workout in the gym. Luckily, Maria only seemed interested in meeting Lady Caroline Hatton, as the barlady had pointed her out as someone she should greet.

"Lady Hatton. I don't think we've met. I'm the owner of Chartridge, Maria Dubois."

"Delighted to meet you. I love what you've done with the old castle. You'll have to give me the name of your interior designer in case I ever get the Hall renovated. This is my very good friend, Hayley Bennett. She's famous in her own right."

"Really? I'm sorry, I don't recognise your name."

"Don't be sorry. I'm more of a local name. I hear you're going to have a psychic weekend."

"However did you know that?"

"I'm psychic."

"How fascinating. You're right, though. My partner and I had thought of having paid weekends, but we hadn't mentioned it to anyone else. Do you think it would work?"

"Absolutely. You could do ghost walks, or ghost hunts. The ghosts would enjoy it too."

"Ghosts? Are you sure?"

"Sir Timothy Whittlebury is behind you, and he's rubbing his hands together. He loves a good haunting. Apparently, you haven't taken much notice of his efforts, though. And there's a rather angry man in a kilt over there, who is not too keen on the idea, but don't worry about him. You've even got Rex, the Irish Wolfhound."

"I can't wait to tell Anita. Mind you, I don't think I'll feel the same in our room. It's always cold and draughty."

"I don't think you've got anything to worry about. You have quite a few resident ghosts, and they haven't hurt anyone yet, have they?"

"That's very true. What exactly do you do, Hayley?"

Lady Caroline answered before she could. "She's amazing. I couldn't believe it when I first saw what she did. She not only sees dead people, she talks to them as well. And Hayley has helped the police on more than one occasion. But that hasn't made her popular, so that's why she can't just go to them about the body."

"Body? What body?"

Hayley said, "There are bones in the grounds here, of a boy. That's what I really needed to talk to you about. Do you know the bench that's in front of Deadman's Pond?"

"I know the bench in front of the lake. I didn't know it was called Deadman's Pond."

"That's the one. We need to move the bench and dig up a young man's bones. If you don't mind."

"Mind? I'd be delighted. Is it like a local, historical legend or something? It would be perfect for the ghost hunts. Can we do it, though? Or do we need the police there?"

"I don't think they'll believe us. And I don't want them to know it's me. So we need to think of something to say."

"I could say I'm building a summer house or something, and then when we find the bones, we could call them. My men could do it very carefully so we won't disturb any evidence. So has he been there for hundreds of years?"

"No. I was sitting on the bench when he told me what he could. He can't remember much, but he counted twelve winters. He has no idea who he is. And that's what we have to find out. As well as find out who buried him alive."

"Oh my. That's rather tragic. But how amazing is that? I'm a great believer in fate. I was going to hire someone to write a whodunit for the murder mystery weekend, but we might have our very own one. I'll do whatever I can to help, Hayley. I suppose once they've got the bones, they can do DNA."

"I really hope so; else we may never find out who Bones is. And they can check the dental records. But there's a detective agency that's looking into it as well, and they're rather good!"

Chapter 16

LILLIAN AND SUZIE ARRIVED AT CHORTLE ACADEMY during the school's lunchtime.

"There they are," said Lillian, pointing to a young black girl, Camille, and her new best friend, Anya. It was Suzie who should have been with Camille, but she was not sorry that Camille had found Anya. In fact, it was she who had made sure that they paired up. It was on the first day at secondary school that they had come across the fragile Anya being bullied for not being able to read in front of the whole class. They both thought that the skinny and shy girl was being neglected, and things were not right at home. And looking at her grubby clothes and dirty hair, they hadn't changed their minds. Lillian noticed for the first time that the blazer, which looked too big, was also for a boy—perhaps from an older brother or given to her by someone else.

There was a deep sadness about the young girl of eleven. When Camille told Anya that her friend Suzie had died on her way to her tenth birthday party, Anya had opened up to say that she had lost her dad when she was eight, so she knew how Camille felt. That must be why she was so sad, they thought.

Friday was PE day for the two girls, and somehow, Anya and

Camille scored the most goals in netball. It was almost like magic that the ball travelled in various directions but always ended up in the net!

Lillian and Suzie decided to follow the girls home to see what home life was like for Anya. Suzie walked home next to Camille as she would have done and felt rather sad when they reached her house. She had spent many hours playing there ever since the two girls had first met in nursery school.

Camille said, "Do you want to come in? Mum's out. I'll make us something to eat."

Much as Anya would have liked to, she said, "No, I'd better not. Mum wanted me to be home on time today." The last time she went in, she didn't want to leave. Everything was so perfect: food in the cupboards and cosy and warm. Besides, if she went inside her house, Camille would have a reason to go to hers. In fact, she had already said those dreaded words, 'Shall I come to your house?' No, she had to keep it to being just friends at school. Mum would go mad if she told anyone anything. But she didn't have to worry about that; as if she would. Anya walked even more slowly after she left Camille. She was in no rush to get home.

The two ghosts and the schoolgirl left the village and came to three small terraced houses just past the pub. The first two looked well-kept, but the far one had an overgrown hedge and weeds. Anya didn't go in the front door but opened the high gate at the side of the house. She knocked on the back door. "Mum, it's only me."

They heard two bolts sliding at the top and bottom and a key turn. Lillian and Suzie looked at each other and frowned.

"Come in quick. How was school?"

"Alright."

"I hope you had your school dinner. I haven't got anything in yet."

"I did, don't worry. Have we got any bread?"

"Half a loaf."

"That's fine. I like toast. Do you want me to do you any?"

"No. I don't want to eat today. I had a lot yesterday."

"Have you heard anything, Mum?"

Her manner changed. "You ask me that every night. I can't stand it." She held her head and sat on the sofa, rubbing the tops of her legs. "It gives me a headache. I can't think of him anymore. I'm going to lie down. Don't look at me like that. Blame your dad."

Anya waited till her mother had gone upstairs and put cartoons on the television to take her mind off what had just happened. The room was a mess, and she had to throw papers and rubbish on the floor to clear a space. It was the same whenever she got back from school. At least it was Friday, and she didn't have to go for a couple of days.

Suzie laid a hand on her shoulder for comfort, but Anya didn't feel a thing.

Lillian thought of Suzie's mother, who was a social worker, and said, "I wonder if we should get Hayley to tell your mum."

"Not until we understand more. There's something wrong with her mum, but did you hear what she said about Anya's dad?"

"That was odd. Anya told Camille that she had lost her dad, and we thought he had died. But perhaps he didn't," said Lillian.

"Maybe they got divorced or he left her after being violent. It could be loads of things. We need to find out more. They both need help by the looks of it. This will have to be our next case. We need Abigail to help unravel it. But we've already got two other cases, so there's no point mentioning it till after the fun run."

Chapter 17

At last, it was the day of the fun run. Hayley hadn't had much sleep, thinking how embarrassed she would be if she couldn't drag her body back to her tent, or even reach the finish line. Maybe she'd pull something and have to be stretchered down the hill. How Tom would laugh. And he was right; she liked to win. Caroline and Isabella will be on their third wine by the time she finishes. Ten kilometres! That was six whole miles. That seemed a long way in a car. What was she thinking? She'd pulled a muscle once bending down to pick up a grape. Hayley put a hand on her chest. Could she die of a heart attack if she wasn't fit enough? That's ridiculous. Old Mrs Smart is doing it, and she's in her seventies. But even she had overtaken her on her run around the village last week.

I'm doing it for the children and babies at the hospital. It might be ours in there one day, she thought. I'll be fine, more than likely. And she had got a lot of sponsors she had talked into giving her money, so she couldn't pull out. Hayley was glad that it looked bright outside. At least it wasn't raining. She looked over at Tom, who was in the bed next to her. He had taken the

Monday off as well, so they had a whole three days together. And it was going to be so much fun camping.

She hoped she hadn't forgotten something important. It was amazing what you had to buy to spend one night in a tent. There was the tent itself, sleeping bags, two stools, a mallet, blow-up mattresses and a lantern. She mustn't forget a torch either. She knew as soon as she got in bed, she would have to get up and go to the toilet. She hated camping already. But she had been feeling so tired lately she could sleep on a clothesline. Must be all that exercising. And they said it was good for you. But she'd better get up. They had to leave at nine.

A few hours later, Luna knew there was something funny going on. The woman next door had popped in, and they had definitely been talking about him. And now they were rushing about and had no time to play. There was a pile of bags and boots by the front door. Now that lady was back. Luna narrowed his eyes. He couldn't understand much of what was being said, but he got the feeling that his man and woman were going somewhere and this other one was going to feed him. Had she been trained? That was the main thing. But it was strange, he was going to miss them and their fussing. He had already made a plan to totally ignore them when they came back. He hoped it wasn't too long. Now to scratch the furniture as well, that would show them.

Polehanger Farm looked totally different as Hayley and Tom arrived. They parked their car in the field that was now signposted and had marshals at the entrance. Then they made their way to the large white marquee, where they showed their ticket and were told where to put up the tent. Melody said hello to Hayley and wished that Penelope was there to help her. But Verity Pikestaff had come early and was being very helpful.

Dave Mills and his wife, Isabella, called them over and told them to put their tent next to theirs. Hayley just hoped she wouldn't snore and keep them awake. She was so pleased when

The Deadly Fun Run

she saw Lady Caroline pull up in her car and the chauffeur open the door for her. Even though she had been asked to start the race as a local celebrity, she was wearing her running gear as well. It had been arranged between them that she, Hayley, and Isabella would run together, and Dave and Tom would start well ahead of them. Isabella's mother was babysitting, and Isabella was so excited to be having a night without interruptions. Even in a tent, she thought she would have a more peaceful sleep.

Hayley had bought a cheap tent at a local shop, and it seemed that an awful lot of the other campers had done the same, including Dave and Isabella.

"How on earth are we going to know which is ours?" said Hayley. "I'm bound to go to the loo in the night. I wouldn't at home, but if I know I can't, I'm sure to have to go."

"I intend to sleep like a log without little Emma to wake me up. Could you tie something on the top?"

"That's a good idea. Give me your shoelaces, Tom."

"I think I'll be needing them. And that won't help you in the dark. You'll just have to count the rows. After all that running, you'll sleep well, believe me."

"You're probably right, hun. And I've brought plenty of beer and white wine."

"So have I," said Isabella. "I'm really looking forward to tonight. The stage looks like a proper festival. Do you know who's performing, Hayley?"

"I know local bands, The Four Mops and Brewers Inc, but then there's a famous surprise group, apparently. I have a feeling it's a well-known old one, but I've no idea who."

"I saw the barbecues as I came in. I'm looking forward to that as well. That's included in the price, isn't it?"

"It's just the marshmallows and the breakfast you have to pay for. Come on, you two boys, hurry and put the tents up."

The tent, which the leaflet claimed could be erected in ten minutes, actually took the two policemen nearly an hour. It wasn't the tent that was the problem, so much as the poles, they explained; the instructions were clearly printed wrong. Eventually, after much swearing, the two tents stood proudly on Sebastian March's farm. Hayley had seen the good-looking man himself wandering around checking on various things, but noticed that he headed for Caroline as soon as he had seen her arrive.

Hayley was surprised, but very pleased that Abigail and the others had not yet arrived. It made it so hard to hear what everyone else was saying with them chattering away in her ears. And she was enjoying having a chat with Isabella about what life was like with a baby. Some things sounded wonderful, and some things would put you off having children for life. Had she really not had a proper night's sleep in nine months! She got cranky when she didn't get eight hours!

She was having such a normal time that she forgot that something awful might happen if Abigail and Terry were right. She hadn't seen Harvey yet, but she tried to keep her eye on Verity, though even she had gone from sight. But then a large motor caravan pulled into the farm, and she heard the butcher bellowing to Melody that he was going to park near the barn and his freezer truck. It was the first time that Hayley had seen Sally Bonson as she got out. She was a tall, well-built lady with a kind face. Her many worry lines could have been caused by being married to her obnoxious husband for many years.

"Shall we do a few stretches?" said Isabella.

"What's the time? I was thinking more of a wine, but you're right. We haven't got that long till kick-off."

"You haven't done one of these, have you?"

"I won't be again either, Isabella. They must have made a lot of money just charging for the tents."

"It's a shame Mrs Ashton-Whyte died. I wonder if CHAF will carry on."

"Murdered, hun. They haven't charged the daughter yet, and

I'm hoping she'll be here today. I think she's meant to say a few words in her mum's memory before the concert starts. She told Penelope that she would." Luckily, Isabella didn't take it in or ask how she could have told her that after she was dead. And that was to be the least of her worries; Abigail had arrived. And she soon shocked Isabella when Hayley shouted out, "What's Bones doing here?"

"Who?" she asked.

"Oh, sorry, Isabella, I've got a skinny friend we call Bones. Oh no, it's not him at all. I'm just popping to the toilet, I won't be long." Hayley took her phone out of her pocket and held it to her ear to speak to Abigail, Terry and Bones.

Abigail said excitedly, "Hayley, we've got so much to tell you."

"Hi, Hayley. It's so nice to leave the castle. And I might be needed to see if I recognise anyone."

"I obviously need to catch up. Hello, Terry. Just you today?"

"The others are coming later on. But now we know this isn't Bones. His name is Elliot Thornton. Celia told us everything."

"We asked her about a Louise and Cheryl, and they both died due to drugs. Listen to this: Louise Wagstaff and Cheryl Bonson. The drugs were supposedly given to them by Louise's boyfriend, Elliot, who disappeared at the same time."

"Of course, it wasn't me, I hope. It must have been someone else who framed and killed me. That's why I came."

Terry said, "We think Verity, Harvey, and whoever told them that the murderer and drug dealer will be here today, are going to get revenge."

Abigail added, "It could be anyone. But it might be something to do with the group that's playing. But whether that person is the murderer or the one they're in cahoots with, we don't know."

"We were trying to solve Penelope's murder, and now we've opened up another case. I'd better not say anything to Tom yet.

I've been trying to keep an eye on Verity, but she keeps disappearing. Harvey and his wife, Sally, have just arrived in that motor van. Why don't you go in there, Abi, and see what they are saying? You might even recognise him, Bones. I mean, Elliot."

"I'd rather you called me Bones. I can't even remember being Elliot. Maybe when I can. I'll see if I know him, and then I'm going to have a walk around. I might see others that I know. But everyone looks so different—the clothes, the hair, and even the cars."

"You enjoy it, hun. We'll be running soon, wish me luck. Are you going to, Abigail?"

"Of course. I want to beat you for a start."

"That's hardly fair. You don't get tired."

"A win is a win. But first I want to go and sit in this fancy caravan and see what the Bonsons are up to. And see what we can get out of them."

After ten minutes, the only thing they got from them was as near as they could get to a headache from Harvey's constant loud voice. Even his long-suffering wife, Sally, offered to go and put the porch up on the motorhome to get a break from him. Bones had no recollection of meeting him, but reckoned that was a good thing.

With two minutes to go, Hayley and Isabella stood on the start line with Lady Caroline, as she welcomed all the runners and then fired the starting pistol. The fun run had begun.

Chapter 18

HAYLEY, CAROLINE AND ISABELLA HAD STARTED running after everyone else, but the three soon began overtaking some of the slower runners. Abigail and Lillian had been right in front of them, but Hayley soon lost sight of the two spirits. They didn't have to worry about people getting in the way.

Betty had volunteered to keep an eye on Harvey Bonson while the others ran, and Terry was watching Melody and Sebastian. Although, they looked too busy to get up to anything much. Suzie was keeping pace with Verity, who was running with some male colleagues from the hospital.

Hayley realised that Caroline and Isabella were no longer beside her, and she felt rather disheartened when some of the older ladies of the village ran past her. She stopped at the first water station and picked up a cup. She probably didn't need it, but it gave her a break. Then she heard a voice from behind her.

"Someone said you might be able to see me."

Hayley looked down and saw a small girl, dressed in a hospital gown. "I can, hun. What's your name?"

"Belinda Taylor."

"I'm Hayley. How old are you?"

"I'm eight and three-quarters."

"And you're very pretty. What can I do for you, Belinda?"

"Mummy and Daddy are running for the hospital today. That's where they last saw me. I just want them to know that I'm alright. They've been so upset for months now and I don't like seeing it. I want them to know that I'm okay, please. And say well done for doing this. I often play at the hospital with the other children and I know they could do with some new toys. The Wendy house is falling to bits. It was there when I first went years ago."

"I'll tell them, and I can put in a word with the organisers. How will I know your parents? There's hundreds of people here today."

"I loved fairies and they're both dressed as one, even Daddy. He's wearing the wings and everything. They aren't far in front, I'll show you."

"Okay. I'll just have my water."

"Hurry up then."

As they ran, Hayley asked her to tell her something about herself.

"We lived in Cadderly. They still do. I was an only child, but they have a baby boy now, called Perry. That's about it. Oh, and I had a bad illness. It was a very long word that began with L. Do you know it?"

"I think I know the one, Belinda. You must have been very brave."

"Not really, it was okay. Mummy and Daddy were braver than me. I didn't mind dying, but they did. I miss the cuddles though. I'd like to have one more before I go. Do you think I could?"

"I'll do my best, but I can't promise, hun. But first we've got to catch them up."

"Can't you run any faster?"

"Probably not, but I'll try for you." Hayley felt a sudden

surge of energy from somewhere to keep up with the little girl. Unlike Abigail, Belinda was weaving in and out of the runners, and checking behind on where she was occasionally. Hayley didn't dare slow down and catch her breath. She didn't even notice that she had passed a surprised Caroline and Isabella. And she could only give a quick wave as she ran past Suzie and Verity as she ran up the steepest part of Chittering Downs.

In almost record time, she had reached the halfway point. The beacon that lit the signals for the next villages in the past, was where she caught sight of a man and a woman dressed in white, and sporting fairy wings. To Hayley, they looked more like angels, if it wasn't for the wands that they were carrying. Luckily they had stopped for water. Hayley stood in front of them, hands on hips, trying to get her breath back.

"Are you… Mr and Mrs… Taylor?" she spluttered.

"Yes," said the woman. "Are you alright? You look like you're about to pass out."

"I feel like it too. Now you need to listen to me, please. I've got a message from someone. I don't know how to say this, but here goes. Belinda wants to say that she's okay and so pleased you're doing this for her children's ward." She didn't give them a chance to interrupt her. "She says can you make sure the hospital gets a new Wendy house, as it's the same one she played in years ago, and it's falling to bits. And she loves the fairy outfits, but where is dad's tiara? She told me she loved fairies. And if you are alright, she's going to go to Heaven." Now Hayley paused, to let them either shout at her, or cry. Fortunately, they did neither.

They held each other and Belinda's mother said, "We knew. When we were getting ready today she was there. We both felt it. I thought I saw my wand move on the bed and I picked it up and made a wish. But I think it was more of a prayer, asking to please let me see my little girl one more time."

"I can't let you see her, But I can let you feel her. She wants one more cuddle with you both before she goes."

Her father spoke for the first time. "I can't believe it, but thank you."

"Let's go over here, out the way." Luckily everyone was too busy running to notice anything. "Put your arm around your wife and Belinda stand here. Now shut your eyes."

"Mike, I can feel her!"

"Me too."

"So can I, Mummy. Our last night night cuddle. For a while anyway."

"Belinda says she can feel you. She says it will be the last cuddle for a while, and to imagine that you're just putting her to bed. And there will be a next time, she promises, when you can all be a family again."

"Thank you, Hayley," said Belinda.

"I'll leave you alone. Goodbye Belinda. It's been very nice meeting you." Mum and Dad still had their eyes closed and were holding their daughter tight, so Hayley slipped away. She started walking slowly down the hill, but turned back to see Mr and Mrs Taylor crying and hugging each other. Little Belinda had gone.

Her walking turned into running to hide the tears that were running down her cheeks. She didn't even know why she felt so emotional. It was a happy occasion for all of them, and she had done it plenty of times. But it was always saddest with a child. Another reason that she was in no hurry to have a baby of her own. How could she cope if she lost him? With blurred vision, Hayley ran past all her friends and villagers. What would have meant so much to her before, was now insignificant after the passing of little Belinda. Before she realised it, the finish line was in sight.

Tom and Dave were sitting on the other side, trying to get their breath back, and they couldn't believe how close she was to their time.

"Blimey, Hayley, I can't believe it. Are you sure you didn't cheat?"

"No I did not! But I did have a good incentive."

"Like a glass of wine and a burger?"

"No, like a gift from God."

Hayley was saved from having to explain by the arrival of Caroline and Isabella.

"Good God, Hayley. I don't believe it," said Caroline.

"It obviously paid off going to the gym with you."

"It must have. We thought we must have been mistaken when you came past us like a train."

"See, nobody thought I could do it. Where there's a will and that. Although talking of wills, I'd better go and have a lie down before I drop down dead. I'm shattered. Must be getting old. I've never felt so exhausted."

"Here, have some water. Shall we go back to the tent?" suggested Tom.

"Good idea, hun. I don't suppose anyone has been attacked or murdered?"

"I think I would have said that if there had been. Why? Were you expecting them to be?"

"Yes and no. Let's go back to the tent and I'll fill you in."

"Okay, saucy. Come on and I'll fill…"

"Not a chance, mate. Like I said, I'm knackered. And I've got to tell you about Bones."

"Bones? As in….?"

"You've got a one track mind. No! I mean the boy that was buried. Then I'm going to sleep, perchance to pass out for half an hour."

"More like lazy bones."

When they got back in the tent, Hayley filled him in on what she knew about Verity and Harvey and their plan, and then about Bones. She didn't really take in what he thought of it all as she had fallen fast asleep.

After a good hour of blissful sleep, Hayley licked her lips and suddenly felt very thirsty. Still with her eyes shut she reached out to feel for Tom on his camp bed.

"What time is it, hun?"

A voice, not Tom's, snapped back, "Time you were up and investigating."

"Abi? What are you doing here? Hi, Betty. Where's Tom?"

"He left about twenty minutes ago. He's outside the tent having a beer with Sergeant Mills and his wife. He thought you looked so peaceful that he left you to it. If Suzie had been here she could have shaken you. You were dead to the world."

"Very funny." Hayley snuggled down in her sleeping bag. "Do you know what it's like to run miles and miles?"

"Piece of cake. I never even broke into a sweat. But how did you do it so fast?"

"Don't tell me, you couldn't believe I finished before you and the others."

"No. I was going to say I thought you must have cheated."

"Well I didn't. Honestly, why is everyone so surprised?"

"Surprised? I'm in shock."

"She hid her light under her bush, as they say, didn't you, Hayley?" said Betty.

"Must have been well hidden," said Abigail laughing. "So how did you do it?"

"I had help from above."

"So you cheated. Told you, Betty."

"I wouldn't quite call it that. But I did have a bit of help."

"I can't believe you're not rubbing my nose in it."

"Nor me. What's going on? Maybe I will later, hun, don't worry. So, what have I missed?"

"Not much actually. Terry is watching the Bonsons. They're just organising the food for the barbecue. Bones is wandering around with Suzie and Lillian somewhere. He hasn't recognised anyone yet. Oh, and Lydia Aston-Whyte is here. She looks so sad. She's spent most of the time talking to Melody. They've been running through what's going to happen on the stage in an hour or so. And her brother Calum is here with his wife. I wonder if he lived here twelve years ago. He'd be about the same age as Bones was. He could be connected to both murders. Verity hasn't done anything suspicious so far."

"What about Sebastian March?"

"I was getting to that. I've got some real goss."

"Do tell," said Hayley, sitting up.

"He and Lady C are looking like quite the couple. Heads together and giggling. A sure sign. I heard her say she was going to stay in the house with him tonight. I'll whip over later and see what they get up to."

"You will not, Abigail Summers. How would that help the investigation?"

"It won't, but it will help me. Don't tell me you're not dying to know what happens."

"Course I am. But I'll do it in a normal way. I'll just keep asking her till she gives in and tells me."

"Please yourself, Hayl. But I don't think she'll be in the spare room."

"Yes she will. She's gentry, don't forget."

"Huh, they're the worst. Remember what all the lords of the manor were like in the past."

"Yes, but not Caroline. She's got her reputation to think of in the county. Anyway, Sebastian is very good-looking, so he's got the pick of loads of women."

"If he's got any sense, he'll go for the one with a title, money and lands."

"So that's another reason she won't move too fast. Is he after her for her money? I can't see the farm making much money. There's a lot of hay and straw, but have you seen a cow?"

"He probably grows potatoes or cabbages, or something."

"Maybe. But Caroline should take her time. I can smell

something's off."

"Well it's not me. I can't even do that anymore."

Hayley laughed. "Actually, I can smell something - sausages. Lovely. I'm starving. Right, look the other way, or go and find Terry. I want to get changed out of my running stuff."

"Don't worry, I'm going. I think I'll go and check on Sebastian. Only to see if he's a murderer of course."

Hayley took off her leggings and t-shirt and put on her comfortable, long skirt and blouse. It wasn't easy in a three-feet high tent. She had forgotten a mirror and brushed her long, black hair, which had been tied back and hoped that she looked alright. Then went to join the others.

"Ah, you're up," said Tom. "You were talking in your sleep." He knew exactly who she was talking to, but didn't want his friends to think his wife was weird. Although both Dave and Isabella already knew she was psychic and helped with the police cases.

"Was I really? That shows how tired I was. Sleeping like the dead!"

Isabella held out a glass of wine. "Here you are. This will wake you up. We'll go and get some food when the queue has gone down a bit."

"Good. Because I could literally eat a horse."

Abigail and Betty found Terry sitting on a bale of hay watching Lydia and Melody. They had both been crying and consoling each other. Betty thought that they would strike up a mother-daughter relationship in the future.

People all around them were tucking into lovely burgers and hotdogs, but the three of them couldn't smell a thing.

"I don't know what to make of Bonson," said Terry. "We're supposed to be working out who murdered Penelope, not wondering if he's going to have a go at someone today. Whatever we're expecting, it could be a red herring."

"I thought he was cooking sausages and burgers," said Betty

seriously.

"Burgers or red herrings, I don't like him one bit. I feel so sorry for his wife. She seems so nice and quiet compared to him."

"I bet she doesn't get a word in longways. Makes me appreciate my John."

"And my Terry," said Abigail, and made his heart swell.

"Why thank you, Abi. That's high praise from you."

"It's true. We need to solve this case and go on another date."

"We could get a train to the seaside," suggested Terry.

"That's a bit ambitious. But I suppose we could."

"I haven't been to the coast for sixty years or more. Since I went to Bognor Regis."

"John and I used to go to Eastbourne. There's a lovely hotel there where all the oldies used to go. We used to feel quite youthful, even if we were in our seventies. Good food though, and they had bingo and a cabaret every night. I wonder if Todd Ray and his little organ are still going. Not that we saw much of it. We used to have a lot of early nights. As you know my John liked to... "

"Well I don't think Todd Ray will be the star attraction tonight, Betty. Have you any idea who it could be, Terry?"

"I heard Melody say that they're expected to arrive after the show starts. They've left a place for the van or coach or something. See, over between the barn and the Bonson's, it says reserved."

"We'll keep an eye out. They'd better hurry up, the first band is getting on stage. I've not heard of them, have you, Betty?"

"The Four Mops? Yes I have. We saw them a few times in Becklesfield Village Hall. They're quite famous around here.They do folk songs and covers. They would get everyone dancing. I don't know the other one."

Terry did. "I think I've heard of them. More country and

western meets punk rock. All I know about the headliners are that they are from the eighties. I bet I know them when I see them."

They decided to move when a couple came and sat on them to get a view of the stage. The other seats soon filled up to see the not-so-famous Four Mops picking up their instruments. Apart from the drummer, there was a guitarist, a man with a tambourine and a lady singer at the front."

Lydia and her brother, Calum, walked onto the stage and silence spread around the campers. Lydia stood at the microphone and looked very nervous.

Her voice broke as she said, "My name is Lydia Aston-Whyte. Our mother was Penelope, who put all this together but sadly died before she could see how well you all did today. She would be so pleased to know how much has been raised already. She worked so hard for her charity and I'm proud to say that so far, nearly ten thousand pounds has been raised for the Children's Ward at Gorebridge General Hospital. So please buy plenty of marshmallows for toasting, and put any change you have in the collection bins. Thank you so much. Now my brother, Calum, will introduce the bands who are giving their time for free tonight."

"I'd like to say thank you to all the people that put this all together and gave their time and money, making this a wonderful day for my mother's legacy. I feel like she is with us today.

But to start the fun part of the fun run, we have the fabulous Four Mops and then the amazing Brewers Inc. But I'd like to announce that the finale will be a group that hasn't done a show for many years, but their music is still selling all over the world today."

Abigail said, "I've just thought, I bet it's Maria Dubois' dad's group, the Dark Brethren. Bet you a million pounds."

"The group doing a special benefit performance tonight is…

The Thorny Issues."

Everyone started clapping and cheering as they walked off stage and the Four Mops started singing. Apart from Abigail.

"I'll take my million pounds now, please, Abigail?"

"Oh, shut up, Terry. The Thorny Issues? I've never heard of them."

"Really?" said Terry and Betty in surprise.

"Huh!" Abigail huffed. "Don't forget I'm much younger than you two."

"Ooh, meow," said Terry.

"Well you know what I mean. Let's go and find Bones and see if he's ever heard of them. I don't know what, but it's got me thinking of something."

They found Bones by the barbecue, wishing he could have a burger. He was with Suzie and Lillian.

"I'm glad you've met Suzie, Bones. She's a Mover. She's great in an investigation. We couldn't have done any of the cases without her. Including yours."

"Cool. She'll be great when we do the haunted nights at the hotel. I'm so looking forward to that."

"Have you remembered anything yet?"

"I've remembered I like burgers. And the Thorny Issues meant something. It made me think of football. Don't ask me why."

"I'm going to though," said Abigail. "Why do you think?"

"I'm listening to them, and I'm on a bed, in my room. Perhaps I was watching football at the same time."

"Hang on. I'm having a bit of a brain wave. What is your real name again, Bones?"

"I think they said it was Elliot Thornton."

"Thornton. I know it's a bit of a stretch, but could the group be named Thorny because somebody named Thornton started it."

"Brilliant, dear."

"Could be," said Terry. "But not necessarily."

"I wish Celia was here. She said Elliot had an older brother. A much older brother, I reckon. She'd know his name, I bet. We'll just have to wait till they get here and see if you recognise anyone."

"I've got a brother. How amazing is that?"

It was at the end of the Four Mops that a large motorhome arrived. It was double the size of the Bonson's. Not many people noticed it, but Harvey Bonson and Verity Pikestaff did. They looked at each other and nodded. Had the person on whom they wanted revenge just arrived? Whatever they had planned for the fun run had commenced.

Chapter 19

AFTER THE SECOND GROUP HAD PERFORMED, MELODY took the microphone and said there would be an interval until the Thorny Issues took to the stage. So to toast some marshmallows and have a drink.

Hayley made an excuse to Isabella and went to find Abigail and the others. She had a dark feeling that one of the group could be responsible for the death of Bones, Cheryl, and Louise, so she was surprised to hear that Abigail thought that one of them could be Elliot's brother. But she was right more times than she was wrong. Abigail also said that he might have supplied the drugs that killed the two young girls.

But Betty wasn't sure that Abigail was right either. "It could just be a coincidence."

"No, I think they got the name of the group from Thornton. I'm as sure as... What's the saying, Betty? As sure as...?"

"Er, it's something to do with chickens. Ducks."

"Near enough. I'm sure, anyway."

"Shall we go over to their van?" asked Lillian. "I went to see them in London years ago."

"You'd better not all go, hun. Lillian, you should go with Suzie. Yes, and you, Abigail."

Inside, their motorhome was more luxurious than most hotel rooms. There were two bedrooms and a large living area. Tuning in a guitar was a long-haired man of about forty. One was sitting at the table smoking a cigarette, and the other was knocking back a bottle of beer.

"Have a look through a few things, Suzie. See if you can see any names."

"Okay, Abi. I can't see anything. It's not like any letters are going to be here. Hang on, there's a bottle of champagne over there with a card. Make sure they aren't looking. I'll have a look. 'To Rob, Ralph, and Dan. Good luck on your comeback'."

"If only Celia was here. We'd know exactly if one of these is his brother."

But they had to get back to the others. The head of the crew entered to tell them that everything was ready for them, and they had ten minutes till they were needed. But was the stage set for music or murder?

Hayley, followed by Betty and Terry, bumped into Harvey and Verity on the way back to Tom, and she struck up a conversation. She introduced herself as a friend of the organisers. "The food was wonderful, Harvey. I ate two burgers and a hotdog, I'm afraid."

"Best meat in the south, lass."

"Definitely. It's gone so well. Penelope would have been so proud of you all."

"It's gone better than we thought," smiled Verity.

"Are you both looking forward to the Thorny Issues? Had you heard of them before?"

They both hesitated, but Verity said, "I seem to remember the name. I can't say I was a fan or anything."

"Didn't one of them have a brother that disappeared? Something to do with drugs, I believe."

"Where did you hear that?" snapped Harvey.

"Oh, someone was saying it. Something Thornton, wasn't it?"

"News to me. Who did you say you were?"

"A friend of Penelope. And Lady Caroline as well. I think you've met her."

"Well, we don't know anything about drugs, or this lad's brother getting murdered. So if you'll excuse me, I've got to get back to my wife."

"Hmm," said Hayley aloud after they walked off. "Who said anything about the brother being murdered?"

"I don't trust him at all," said Betty. "I rather hope it was him that killed Penelope. Give his poor wife a rest. I can't see it being any of the others. Not that I've met Sebastian March yet."

"He's rather good-looking, Betty. You'll like him."

"Oh, don't you girls start all that again. You know, when you go all googly-eyed."

"I've never gone googly-eyed in my life," said Hayley. "Apart from you-know-who at the regatta."

"Oh yes. I went a bit googly then. Made me wish I was sixty years younger. And alive. He had the biggest…"

"Thank you, Betty."

"I was going to say muscles. Now my John, he had the biggest…"

"Oh good, there's Caroline and Sebastian. I'll go and say hello."

"Hello, Hayley. We're just going to see the group. How do you feel now? A bit achy?"

"I must admit I had a bit of a nap. Hi, Sebastian. The farm looks great. It's going so well, isn't it?"

"It is. And everyone is being well-behaved. I can't say I'll be sorry when it's over, mind you."

"I should imagine there'll be a lot of cleaning up tomorrow. Are you looking forward to the Thorny Issues? I can't believe

Penelope got them to play in little old Becklesfield. I wonder if they come from here."

"Not that I know of. Yes, I'm surprised. But perhaps they have a connection to the hospital. That's what it's all about, don't forget."

"Maybe. Do you know the lead singer's name?"

Sebastian shrugged. "I haven't got a clue. I wasn't a fan. Why?"

"I thought I recognised him. Never mind. So are you camping out, Caroline?"

"Er, Sebastian has kindly got a room ready for me in the farmhouse."

Hayley smiled at them. "That's very kind of you. I don't suppose you've got one for me."

"And deprive you of the chance of camping under the stars."

"I'm only kidding. I'm sure I'll sleep like a baby tonight."

Melody's voice filled the air. "Ladies and gentlemen, please put your hands together for our guests of honour. Back for one last performance - The Thorny Issues."

Applause, cheers, and whistles drowned out the opening notes as the three men started to play. Hayley found Tom, and he put his arm around her as they both watched.

"They are good, aren't they," shouted Hayley. The volume was much louder than with the other two bands.

"I do remember them now. I loved this song."

"Abigail thinks one of them might be Bones' brother. Can you look into them when you go back to work for us?"

"That's not till Tuesday. And I can't exactly get Dave to do it. I can't say that a dead journalist told us that he went missing after being suspected of killing two girls."

"He guesses what I do."

"But whether he believes it is a different thing. I'm sure it can wait a few days. He's been dead for twelve years, so it's hardly life or death."

The Thorny Issues finished their set to a standing ovation. Abigail wasn't sure what she expected to happen, but nothing did. Bones had watched the show, and it hadn't brought back any memories or recognition of any of the men.

The spirits watched as the Breathers went to their tents and settled down for the night. The fire was dying, but they sat around to discuss what had or hadn't happened.

"It feels like such an anti-climax," said Betty sulkily. "I was expecting at least a punch-up between Harvey and someone. What was it you and Terry heard him say to Verity?"

"Something like, not long to wait, and that something was going to happen at the fun run, and would he be there. Should we warn Hayley and Tom?"

Lillian said, "No, let her sleep. You've already woken her once today. She needs her sleep. It can wait."

"Okay. Shall we go back to the library?"

"Can't we stay here?" said Suzie. "I'm enjoying it. And Bones is, aren't you?"

"Makes a change from the hotel. Let's tell ghost stories like we used to when I was in the Scouts."

"You had another memory, Bones."

"So I did. I went to Scouts."

"Trouble is, ghost stories won't be scary for us. Let's tell people stories," said Betty. "I used to love a good slasher movie."

"I wouldn't have thought you would like horror films, Betty. I've got just the one," said Terry. "It all started December 31st, 1999."

"Millennium night," said Abigail.

"Yes. It was an odd time. The end of another century. There were many people that thought that it would be the end of the world. They thought all technology would come to a halt because of the change of years. Or that God would destroy the earth. But the town clock struck twelve, and Becklesfield and the world carried on as before.

Now in those days, there was a manor house called Bogmires Grange. An old spooky mansion that's since been knocked down, and Harts Nursing Home has been built on the grounds. That's full of ghosts, but that's another story.

Sir Richard Brindle lived there then, and he threw a New Year's party there every year. For the millennium, he decided to do something special and make it fancy dress. I'd watched them all make their way there from the village. It was only a twenty-minute walk up Birdwalk Lane. There were martians, cowboys, elves, and some rather sexy bunny girls.

But just past midnight, I saw a young couple come towards me as I sat on the churchyard wall. The moon was full, so I could make them out quite well. He was a pirate with a sword through his belt, and the girl was an air hostess, in a light blue suit and hat. Anyway, they were arguing. She accused him of not being there at midnight for her kiss and to say happy New Year. He said it wasn't his fault; someone had grabbed him and planted a kiss on his lips and wouldn't let go. This made it worse as she said she thought he'd been with his mates, not kissing some strange woman. But things got heated, and she told him to get lost, and so he stormed off up the high street, and she walked towards her house.

The girl didn't seem too bothered, but she suddenly stood still and listened. She swung around, but no one was there. She shrugged and went on a few more steps but stopped again, and this time we both heard the dull thud of footsteps coming from the dark. Then we heard a deep, husky voice whisper, 'Jennifer, Jennifer.'

It frightened the life out of me, I can tell you. So Jennifer, as I now knew, shouted out, 'Who's there? I mean it, if that's you, Jack, I'm going to kill you'.

But there was no answer. Just the sound of heavy breathing

and a mist from their breath. So she turned and started to run, but she had high-heels on, and so she stumbled more than once. The footsteps got faster and heavier. And a disembodied growl said, 'I'm coming for you, Jennifer.'

I didn't know whether to charge at the voice or stay with the terrified girl. But there wasn't much I could have done, as you know. Then I saw the figure and stopped dead at the dreadful sight."

Suzie snuggled up to Lillian.

"I saw a figure dressed in black. Wild hair and nearly six feet tall. It took me a minute to realise that it was a woman dressed as a witch. And held on high, in black, lace fingerless gloves, was a long-bladed knife glinting in the moonlight.

I implored Jennifer to run faster, but she was no match for the wild woman. I stood in front of her, but I was powerless. The long knife struck her in the back. Not once, but twice. The witch disappeared into the night, and I had to watch as the blood ran out of her young body."

Suzie gave a shiver, and Bones put his arm around her.

"Well, before many seconds had passed, Jennifer was standing next to me, looking down at her own body. She simply said, 'I'm too young to die. I shouldn't be here.' Then we heard the sound of someone running towards us. Her boyfriend had returned after being worried about her. He screamed her name and for help when he saw her, and took off his pirate's jacket and pushed it down on her wounds to stem the flow of blood. He begged her not to die and to come back to him."

"And did she?" said a worried Betty.

"I could see her aura fading in and out. She wasn't going to make it. So I said to her, 'Go back. It's not your time.' The words of her boyfriend had saved her; she wanted to stay with him. I said to her, 'Tell them you were killed by a witch, who was in black, and wearing black, lace fingerless mittens. She put the knife in the boughs of the yew tree in the graveyard. Go now.'

She gave me a heavenly smile and returned to her body. And Jack held her in his arms till help arrived.

Well, Jennifer married her pirate, and they now have three children. Mary Prescott was charged with attempted murder and is still in prison. She vows revenge on the poor girl from her cell. She still doesn't know how Jennifer could swear in a court of law that she turned and saw who attacked her, as she knew that she was already face down and looking the other way when she hid the knife high in the tree. She swears a deadly vengeance on the one that took her Jack from her. Hadn't he sworn his love and loyalty when he kissed her on Millennium night at the strike of the hour? I've heard her sentence is up this very week. Jennifer and Jack will never be safe till the day she dies. Every New Year's Eve, they check all the doors and windows and keep a vigil in case the wild witch returns for another midnight kiss. The end."

"Brilliant, Terry," said Lillian. "But is it true?"

"Of course it's true. Would I lie to you?"

"Well...," started Abigail.

"If you don't believe me, ask Celia Hanson. It was a big case all those years ago."

"I think I remember it," said Betty.

"I'll still check with Celia."

Lillian said, "Are you sure it's not that you've had your nose put out of joint. Jealous because Terry was solving crimes way before you, Abigail?"

"Me? Jealous? I haven't got a jealous bone in my body," said Abigail, blinking very quickly. This got the others giggling.

"Well, maybe a small bone or two," she admitted begrudgingly.

"Can we have another story, pleeease, Terry? I loved it," begged Suzie.

"Alright, love. Hopefully, this one won't scare you too much. Now when I was young, everyone knew about the Blue Lady.

She haunted this very stretch of road. Her real name was Lady Katherine Manton. She was travelling back from the Midsummer Ball that used to be held at Chiltern Hall. She was with her husband in their carriage when it was stopped by the famous highwayman, Alfred Snooks. He was actually hanged right here. It's been called Polehanger Farm ever since. But that wasn't until many years after my story.

The masked man was on his dapple grey steed, and he forced the terrified couple to alight from the safety of the carriage. While holding his flintlock pistol against his wife's head, he took Lord Manton's money and pocket watch. But Lady Katherine refused to give up her golden locket, which was a gift from her deceased parents. In a struggle to wrestle it from her neck, his pistol went off, and she was shot. On a night like this, if you listen carefully, you can still hear the sound of horses' hooves and the sound of a scream as Lady Katherine Manton falls to the ground. Listen…"

Terry cupped his hand by his ear for dramatic effect, not knowing that a spine-chilling scream would shatter the quiet, and send terror through the campers at Polehanger Farm.

All the spirits were the first to arrive at the barn from where the scream had seemed to come. They saw Lydia Aston-Whyte kneeling down by a body with a look of horror on her face.

Standing above them both was Hayley Moon, who said, "He's dead."

"Oh my God. It wasn't me, I swear. I just found him."

Hayley helped the shaking girl to her feet. "I know, hun. But it's not going to look good for either of us. Johnson will be overjoyed."

It was then that she noticed Abigail and the others watching her from the door. "Did any of you see anything? It's my friends, Lydia."

"No. We were sitting around the fire, how annoying. Tell us quickly what happened, before everyone comes."

"I got up to go to the loo and got here just after Lydia found the body. Whoever did it had gone."

"Who is it? Thornton?" asked Abigail.

"No. It's Sebastian March."

Chapter 20

DETECTIVE CHIEF INSPECTOR TONY JOHNSON HATED being woken up. Especially on a Saturday night, at gone three o'clock. Or the witching hour, as his ex-wife called it. And she should know, he thought. It didn't help that he had met up with a few of his more shady acquaintances, and they'd bought him far too many whiskies in the Red Lion.

Luckily, the desk sergeant had the sense to send a uniformed police constable to take him to the scene of the crime. He knew there would be no chance that the DCI would be under the legal limit for driving.

Johnson leant back in the passenger seat and closed his eyes. All he knew was that a body had been found at the fun run and campout. That was two murders connected to that now. First that Aston-Whyte woman and now someone else. The Chief Constable wasn't going to be best pleased. He remembered that Mills and Bennett were running on behalf of the police. Useless gits, letting something happen on their watch. That weird Bennett woman better not be there this time, poking her long witch's nose into things that don't concern her. Nah, he couldn't be that unlucky again, surely.

By the time he arrived at the scene of the crime, officers had put up the yellow tape, and the body was being photographed. But that hadn't stopped a crowd gathering to get a glimpse of the gory sight. Some were even taking photos on their phones. Johnson barged his way through, knocking the phones out of hands as he went. The first person he saw was PC Bennett, which didn't help his mood at all. Tom held up the tape and ignored the scowl.

"Bennett, get these gawpers out the way. Mills, tell me what's happened. Then pray to God that it's not an accident and you've got me out of me comfy bed for nowt."

"Definitely murder, sir. The doctor has just left and confirmed the cause of death, and says he'll do the postmortem tomorrow. Seems a length of guy rope had been tied to these two tent pegs either side of the door, and the victim tripped as he came into the barn. Looks like he turned to look up and someone hit him on the head with this."

Sergeant Mills held up a black rubber mallet in a plastic bag and pointed to the victim. A red circle stood out on the skin of his forehead. The eyes were open in fright, as if he saw the blow coming.

"Great. So we've death by mallet, tent pegs, and guide ropes."

"Guy, not guide, sir."

"Whatever. I'm saying it's not going to be easy in a field of campers, is it? How many tents are there here?"

"About fifty, give or take."

"So we need to go round every tent, take names and see their mallets."

"Not every tent will have one, sir. And I bet there's a lot that forgot to bring one. Like me. We had to borrow Tom's."

"So who is the victim? Do we know?"

"The owner of the farm, Sebastian March."

"And who found the body?"

"Ah, well, you may remember her, sir, Lydia Aston-Whyte."

"Did she, by George."

"But, erm, someone else you know found her kneeling by the body."

"Please don't tell me she's got long, black hair, looks like a hippy and thinks she's a witch."

"I won't, but it is, I'm afraid. How did you know?"

"I had an awful feeling. Maybe she's not the only psychic. And where are the two guilty parties? This could be the shortest investigation ever."

"They're in the victim's house. In the kitchen."

"Why the hell did you let them in there? Then again, at least I can get a drink while I grill—I mean, question—them. Come on, let's go. Let's leave the CSIs to do their job."

Abigail and the others had split up. Terry and Betty had gone to check where Harvey, Verity, and Melody were. Lillian, Bones, and Suzie had gone to spy on the Thorny Issues, but they were all fast asleep, knocked out by all the drink they had consumed, judging by all the empty bottles that were on every surface of the van. But that didn't mean that Ralph, Dan, or Rob hadn't killed Sebastian, and then gone to bed for an alibi.

Abigail had gone straight to the farmhouse to check that Lady Caroline was alright. She was in bed in the spare room, flicking through her phone, oblivious to the fact that her host—and more likely her boyfriend—had even left the house. That was, not until Hayley and Lydia arrived in a state of panic, accompanied by a policewoman.

When Johnson and Mills walked into the kitchen, they saw Hayley, Lydia, and Lady Caroline Hatton sitting at the pine table, sipping a hot drink. Obviously not Abigail, who was sitting next to Hayley. A brown blanket had been put around Lydia's shoulders, her eyes were red, and her hands were still shaking. They shook even more when she saw who had arrived to question her.

Lady Caroline was the first to speak. "DCI Johnson, can I get you both some tea? They say it's good for shock."

Mills thought he'd be more shocked if he said yes. He wasn't wrong.

"Mills will, but make mine a bit stronger, please, ma'am. Medicinal purposes. I've had a bit of a chest, and this damp air isn't helping."

"Sherry, Inspector?"

Johnson looked like he had been hit on the head with a mallet. "Sherry? You haven't got anything a wee bit stronger than that, have you?"

"Whisky?"

"Perfect. So, Miss Aston-Whyte, I hear you found the body. Why had you arranged to meet Sebastian March in the barn?"

"I didn't even know him. So I definitely wasn't going to meet him."

"But you were found kneeling by the body, weren't you? So what else were you doing there?"

"I saw a light on in the barn, so I went in and tripped over something. Then I saw him and screamed."

"That's when I found her," said Hayley.

"So I hear, Mrs Bennett. And tell us why you and this girl just happened to be wandering around in the middle of the night. Or was there a meeting of the coven?" he said, laughing at his own joke.

"Very good, Tony. Well, in my case, I needed the loo, that's all. And I saw Lydia and wondered what she was doing, so I followed her."

"I couldn't sleep. I kept thinking about my mother dying. I was going mad in the tent on my own. Calum was going to stay, but he went home in the end after the concert. I was going to sit by the fire, but then I saw the light and I went to see if there was anyone in there that I knew."

"Hmm. Not too convincing, is it? So last time it was a cat, do you think a cow lured him in here?"

Abigail said to Hayley, "He really is a sarcy little sh—"

"She said no such thing. It was you that said that," said Hayley quickly.

"But it is funny that two people have died, and both times you were there within minutes."

"That is true, actually," agreed Abigail, which Hayley ignored, but even she thought it was a big coincidence.

"We don't know when he was killed yet, sir."

"Thank you, Mills, you're not helping. Can you think of who would want to kill your mother and this farmer? I'm pretty sure it must be the same person. We need to check his will, Sergeant, maybe he's left everything to her as well."

"I told you I didn't know him."

"But we've only got your word for that. Give your phone to Mills, please. Seems to be a regular occurrence, if I'm not mistaken. I've a good mind to arrest you here and now, Lydia, and save a lot of time and effort," Johnson said to the already shaking girl.

Abigail shook her head. "He really is a complete ba—"

"But you need a lot more proof than that," said Hayley, ignoring Abigail.

"Leave it to the professionals, please. So when did you last see him, Lady Caroline? And what exactly are you doing here?"

"Sebastian was a friend, and he kindly gave me a room for the night. I was the guest starter for the fun run."

"I will still need your whereabouts and a statement, please."

"We went to bed, separately, just before twelve. We had both had an early start, and I had taken part in the fun run. So I was extremely tired by then."

"Did you hear him leave? And you say you were in separate rooms," Johnson said with a knowing wink at her. "I suppose you need to keep up appearances."

"I don't lie, Inspector. Just ask your Chief Constable."

"Just answer the question, please. Name-dropping won't help you."

"I heard nothing at all, Inspector. I was fast asleep."

Abigail said to Hayley, "That's not true, she was on her phone when I got here."

"Did he get a phone call? Did he say he was going to meet anyone?"

"Not a word. And he could have done, there was no relationship between us. And no, I didn't hear his phone ring. But I have got one thing to tell you. I was in the barn earlier this evening with Sebastian. He was showing Melody Myatt where her helpers could put the hired tables and chairs till the morning, and I noticed the two metal tent pegs either side of the door. I have no idea why. I just thought that was a strange place for someone to have banged them in."

"But no rope?"

"No rope or mallet," Caroline told him. "And I didn't think it was worth mentioning to Sebastian. Obviously, I wish I had now."

Hayley said, "So this was highly planned, Tony. If either Lydia and I had planned it to that extent, surely we would have made sure we were elsewhere when the body was found."

"Maybe you didn't expect Lydia to be there. And maybe you didn't expect Hayley to turn up, so you let out a scream. You know what they say about best-laid plans and mice, or something. And no, miss, I won't be looking for a mouse instead of a cat this time," which he thought was very clever, but carried on when no one else smiled.

But Abigail did say, "Don't give up the day job. Mind you, he should."

"Okay, that will be all for now. But you will both have to come to the station tomorrow."

"Would it be alright if I took Lydia back to Chiltern Hall for the night? She's obviously still suffering from shock. We won't skip the country."

"I suppose so. I'll arrange for a car to take you."

"That's very thoughtful of you, but I've already rung for my chauffeur to collect us. He's on his way."

Mills and Johnson left the ladies and went out into the dark farmyard. "Bloody chauffeur. I wish I had someone to drive me round like Lady Muck."

"Didn't PC Jones pick you up tonight, sir?"

"Don't push it, lad. I've earned the privilege by hard graft, not by being born into it with a silver spoon up my whatsit. Right, so young Lydia has means and opportunity. We just need to find the motive. Good-looking bloke, could be jealousy. We need to find out if she has a temper, and talk to any old boyfriends that have complained about her behaviour. Okay, check for mallets but don't take details till the morning, it's too dark. I'm going home to get my beauty sleep. Where's that driver? Secure the scene after forensics have gone, and make sure that idiot Bennett doesn't leave it unattended till his relief in the morning. And don't let any campers leave, especially that Hayley woman."

But Hayley had no intention of going anywhere. She told Abigail to round up the others and meet at her tent for a meeting of The Deadly Detective Agency.

Chapter 21

BY THE TIME THE INSPECTOR HAD KNOCKED BACK A nightcap and got in bed, Hayley was in her tent sitting opposite Terry, Betty, and Abigail. The others had gone back to the library as there wasn't much they could do till first light. All the suspects were now in their beds or camp beds. None of them had shown signs of guilt when they had been woken by the scream or the police.

Betty wanted to know how Lady Caroline had taken the news.

"She's not too bad, hun. They haven't known each other for more than a few weeks."

"Sometimes that's all it takes, dear."

"That's true. There was definitely a spark between them. She doesn't seem to have much luck with men."

"But I'm guessing this is the first time that one of them has been hit on the head with a mallet," added Terry. "Where's your mallet, Hayley?"

"Don't worry, I checked. It's in the boot. I think they're going to check them all for DNA and blood tomorrow. Although I didn't see any blood on the body. Just a big circle on his forehead." Hayley gave a shudder. "He has passed, I think. I did see one Dead. But from the seventeen hundreds."

"I bet that was Lady Katherine Manton," said Betty excitedly, to which Abigail rolled her eyes.

"I'm not sure who that is, but it wasn't actually."

"Told you," said Abigail.

"No, it was a highwayman."

"Haha. Alfred Snooks. That had you, Abi. Told you. But we haven't seen Sebastian either. So you're probably right," Terry answered.

"Shame. Because he must have been looking up into the eyes of his killer."

Betty said, "Poor man. He was powerless on the floor. I'm thinking he must have been told to meet someone and they put the rope there ready."

"Could have been anyone, hun. I'm thinking of a woman like Verity. He could have overpowered her, so she had to make sure that he wasn't in a position to fight back."

Abigail frowned. "Or an older, fatter man. Sebastian March was young and fit. I tell you what I did notice and Johnson didn't: March was wearing the same clothes as he did this afternoon. So he obviously had no intention of going to bed like he told Caroline. Whoever he met, they must have arranged it earlier on. And we know nothing about that group. They were drunk as skunks, so one of them could have needed a bit of help to down him. And they had arrived early enough. We need to find out from Tom what their names are. We have no idea if we're right yet about one of them being Bones' brother. We only know their first names."

"Actually, I can look on my phone. Here it is. *The Thorny Issues* are an English rock and pop band formed in 1989. Original members are Don Brent, Rob Kingsley, and drummer... Now don't let it go to your head, Abi, but you might be right. Drummer and songwriter is Ralph Thornton."

Abigail was obviously delighted, but merely said, "It was just a guess. Any of you could have said the same. A bit of luck actually. Hayley, you'll need to have a chat with everyone. They won't be able to leave right away. Someone must have a connection to those two dead girls."

They all froze as the tent zip was lifted. Hayley breathed a sigh of relief when she saw it was only Tom.

"Sorry, did I frighten you? Who are you talking to? Actually don't tell me. I just wanted to tell you, and I'm guessing Abigail, that the fingerprints show that the dead man wasn't Sebastian March, but someone called Francis Walker. Gotta go. Me and Jane have to keep watch in the barn all night. I just wanted to check that you were okay." With the sound of the tent zip going down, Tom was gone.

Terry said, "I think Celia mentioned a Francis Walker as a suspect for the drugs, but he had an alibi."

"You're right, she did. But let me think." Abigail put her head back, and as she often did, began moving her hands as if she was moving chess pieces.

Betty whispered, "She's having another brainwave. Hold onto your hats."

"Not a brainwave, more of a ripple at the moment. I'm just thinking that name seems familiar somehow. Not just with Celia. And if it does, it might explain a piece of the puzzle. But I could be wrong. But if I'm right, I know why Penelope was murdered and by who."

"Goodness, I forgot all about her," admitted Betty. "Do you think there will be any more murders?"

"I don't think so. This is about revenge, pure and simple. We need to let Hayley get some sleep. Even in this light I can tell you look a bit peaky."

"I do feel shattered. And a bit sick. I'm wondering if I got a dodgy burger."

"So you go to sleep, and we'll wake you at about eight.

You've got to go to the police station and give a statement at some point, but first you've got to go and talk to a certain person, who'll tell you everything we need to know."

"Who?" they all asked.

"Ralph Thornton, of course."

Chapter 22

THE CURTAINS WERE STILL SHUT WHEN HAYLEY AND Abigail knocked more than once at the motorhome of the famous group. A gruff voice shouted out to get lost. Abigail went in and said the drummer was lying on a seat. But after more knocking, the door opened a crack. It was Ralph Thornton.

"My name is Hayley. I need to talk to you, Ralph."

"I don't talk to fans."

"I'm not a fan."

"Then get lost before I call security."

"Say the name Francis Walker, Hayley." But he still tried to shut the door. "Tell him I know you're responsible for the death of Penelope Aston-Whyte."

The door opened fully as soon as Hayley repeated the words, and Ralph stood to one side to let her into the van that stank of stale cigarette smoke and beer. He was a tall, thin man of about fifty. His greying hair was swept back, showing a widow's peak.

"Come in. Excuse the mess. Sit down," he said as he threw his blanket and pillow on the floor. "I sleep in here, Dan and Rob have the bedrooms. Don't worry about them. They don't come out of a coma till midday. Hayley, was it? So what the hell are you on about?"

Hayley wasn't sure herself, so she just parroted what Abigail was telling her, pausing from time to time when she was shocked at what she was saying.

"I know you've heard about the owner's death, because the police went round to everyone last night and told you not to leave. But you recognised Sebastian March, didn't you? He had been in the media as a benefactor for the fun run. You knew he wasn't Sebastian March, but a thug called Francis Walker. He disappeared after the death of two girls. And we know that you were responsible for poor Penelope's death and more than likely his."

"I still don't know what you're on about, love. I don't know any Penelope." But as he lit a cigarette, his hand shook.

"You sent Penelope two or three emails. All from the same company. It was clever to use a fictitious pharmaceutical company, which you called Walker and Francis. They were offering a large donation or services. You knew she'd probably tell the others on the committee. You wanted to send him a warning that you knew who he was, and wanted to make him suffer. But he thought Penelope had recognised him, so he thought she was blackmailing him. Probably in the next breath, she asked for more money. But she was totally innocent, wasn't she? He followed her home from the meeting at the Cricketers and pushed her off the ladder to her death."

"Say I did send her the emails, how could I have known that he would kill her? I can't be arrested for anything. And anyway, I heard it was an accident. You have no proof at all."

"But we know that someone got in touch with Harvey and Verity to tell them. They had no idea who March really was. And of course, their names meant nothing to him. He couldn't care who died from his drugs. And anyway, they told me it was you that told them," lied Hayley.

"So they opened their big mouths. I knew I should have done it on my own."

"Done what, Ralph? Kill Sebastian March? How did you know for sure it was him? It's been twelve long years."

"I knew. I'd never forget. I've looked for him wherever I've gone. In the faces of crowds. He was a flash git. Still is. Always dropping French words like he was so clever. So when I saw his face and saw the name, I knew. March, French for walk. What? I went to grammar school. And Sebastian. Huh, that was so like him. He hated his name."

"Francis?"

"He wished. Everyone called him Frank. Drove him up the wall. Trust him to pick something pretentious like Sebastian. But I didn't kill him. Us three were going to corner him today. We were going to shove him in Verity's car boot and take him somewhere quiet. Have a friendly chat and find out what he did to Harvey's granddaughter and Verity's sister when they died. But what you don't know is that I needed to find out what happened to my baby brother, Elliot. He was Louise's boyfriend and they died of Walker's lousy drugs. But he disappeared and everyone blamed him. But I knew he hated drugs and loved Louise. He would never have left her to die. I owe it to Mum to clear his name and find him. She thinks he'll walk in the door one day, but I think Walker did something to him. He would have been in touch. I had to know. I wouldn't kill the bastard. I intended to torture him till he told me. Me and Mum will never know now. But you wouldn't know that before you pass judgement."

"Oh, but I do."

"How could you?" he scoffed as he dropped the cigarette into a can of lager.

Hayley took his hand. "I'm so sorry. Elliot told me. I have some sad news for you. I should have said before, I know so much because I'm a psychic medium. I've seen Elliot. I'm so sorry; he's dead."

He slammed the table with his fist. "I knew it. It was Walker, wasn't it?"

"Elliot's not sure, but it probably was. He can't remember anything before he died, because we believe that Frank Walker hit him on the head and buried him in the grounds of Courtridge Castle."

Ralph put his head in his hands. "I knew he wouldn't just leave us."

He straightened up and wiped his face. "Is he okay? Is he here? Can you let me talk to him?"

"Elliot isn't here, but I know where we can find him. The castle is a hotel now. I was in the garden and saw him on a bench. He's perfectly happy. As soon as I can, I'll meet you there, and you and your mother can talk to him. He can't remember much, but he can remember something about football."

Ralph smiled for the first time. "I used to take him to all the matches. Our dad died young, so I did what I could before I toured with the band."

"More may come back when he can talk to you."

"That's if I'm not arrested once you've told all this to the police."

"My husband is a police constable, but he's off duty now, and I won't be helping the man that's in charge."

"Who do you think killed Walker? As I said, it wouldn't have been Harvey and Verity. Not yet anyway. Mum never leaves the house, and I haven't mentioned that I saw Walker to her. I bet he's made a lot of enemies over the years. I wouldn't be surprised if he hadn't bought this farm as a way of laundering his drug money. He could even grow his own marijuana here. There's plenty of heavies in Gorebridge that wouldn't like him selling on their territory."

"But he wouldn't have gone to meet them in the middle of the night. And they would have picked a time when there weren't all these people about. We know someone that loved Penelope very much. Actually, three people. Her daughter, son, and a lady called Melody Myatt. Have you heard of her? She worked with Penny for years and never told her that she had feelings for her. Maybe she found out that he had killed her somehow. I'm really hoping it was a thug from his past. If you recognised him, there's a chance that someone else did."

"I'm so sorry about that Penelope woman. If I'd have known, I wouldn't have said anything. I was just trying to wind him up. It might not have been him. Maybe there's only one killer and they killed them both for some reason."

"That's not likely, but I'm sure the police will look into that."

"Maybe it's someone going around killing members of the fun run."

"Like you, you mean," said Hayley. "Though, I don't get the feeling that it is."

Abigail said, "It's not, Hayley."

Ralph was surprised when Hayley looked to her left and said, "Do you know who killed Sebastian, Abi?"

"I do. But I wished that I didn't. And that's not like me. Let's get back to the others. I need to check a few things first."

"Ralph, trust me for now. Take my card if you need me, and I'll be in touch soon. Please don't mention me to the police. You can say that you recognised Walker if you want, but I'd keep everything else to yourself."

Ralph looked at the card after she had gone.

The Deadly Detective Agency
All Problems Great & Small
Paranormal & Normal

There was an email address for Hayley Moon. He lit another cigarette and found a bottle with some beer still in it. As soon as he could leave, he needed to go and see Mum. She would be broken-hearted, but it had to be done. She had to know that her lovely boy wouldn't be home again.

Chapter 23

ONCE TOM HAD LEFT FOR WORK, HAYLEY AND ALL THE members of the agency gathered in Hayley's conservatory. On the way back from Polehanger Farm, Hayley had picked up Bones.

"We've learned so much, we just had to tell you," said Hayley. "We know everything now. We know who your brother is. And thanks to Abigail, we know who killed you, Penelope, and Sebastian March."

"So all the deaths are connected to mine."

"Not just yours, hun. There's two more as well. They were the catalyst for this. Shall I tell him, Abigail, or do you want to?"

"You know me, I'm easy," which made the others smile. "You go ahead," she said, frowning at Terry, who blew her a kiss.

"If you're sure. Okay, so you had a girlfriend, Bones. A lovely girl called Louise Pikestaff."

"Louise. I can't remember her, but carry on."

"She had a friend called Cheryl Bonson. She was a bit younger. They were both given a contaminated ecstasy pill."

"It wasn't me."

"We know, hun. Cheryl was in Gorebridge Hospital before

she passed, but your Louise died more or less straight away, and you disappeared that night. You might have confronted the drug dealer, we don't know. But whatever you did got you murdered by an evil man called Francis Walker."

"I can't think of him."

"He was often called Frank."

"Frank? As you said his name, I felt someone walk over my grave."

"That could be your subconscious telling you. By all accounts, he was a nasty piece of work. And you were right about the football. We know for sure now that your brother is Ralph Thornton, drummer of the Thorny Issues. He said he used to take you to matches."

"I knew it. I can practically picture it. I'm getting closer." Bones went quiet. "Can you tell him where I'm buried, please?"

"I already have. We're meeting him there, and he's bringing your mother."

"Thank you, Hayley. I can die happy now."

"And Elliot, they hadn't stopped looking for you all these years. But it will give them closure. Especially if I can get the owner to find your remains. Maybe even the police will do that now. Then you can have a proper burial."

"So do you know where this Frank Walker is now? I need to know that he'll get his comeuppance."

"He's already been comeuppanced," said Betty. "Someone hit him in the face with a mallet."

"That was him?"

Abigail had kept quiet as long as she could. "Yes. He came back here under the name of Sebastian March!"

"The one that was friendly with Lady Caroline?" said Suzie. "Poor Caroline."

"I would say lucky Caroline. Imagine if she had married him. He was obviously trying to worm his way into her affections. If he had become Lord of the manor, I should imagine it wouldn't be long before she had an accident."

"Yes, he'd already done one murder, plus those two girls," said Terry.

"Two," said Abigail, to everyone's surprise, except Hayley. "He killed Penelope. Unfortunately, your brother had tried to send a message to him that he knew who he really was. He pretended to own a drug company called Walker and Francis. But Penelope talked about the firm more than once, and Sebastian thought that she was on to him. He feels awful about it, of course. And there was no way he could have known the consequences. Getting back to his death, we heard Harvey and Verity arranging to meet someone in revenge for the two young girls."

Lillian said, "No, you're wrong. Verity's tent was by the campfire when we were telling stories. We would have seen her if she was out and about. And those tent zips could wake the dead, let alone the ones that are awake. So that leaves Harvey Bonson."

Hayley shook her head, "Not him either. As I walked past his van, I heard him snoring. Again, loud enough to wake the dead and the living."

"So who killed Sebastian if it wasn't those two?" asked Suzie.

Betty gave the answer which she always gave. "A drug deal gone wrong."

"Not their MO," said Hayley. "And it wasn't Ralph, not before he'd beaten the truth out of him to find out what he'd done to you."

Suzie said, "I bet Abigail knows. She's just like Miss Marple."

"Do you mean old and a spinster," joked Terry.

"Ha ha, very funny. No dates for you."

"I'm sorry, darling. Love you."

"Hmm. Good job I've got a good sense of humour. But, yes,

Suzie, I do know. And I'm a bit sad about it. She has the means, motive, and opportunity."

"Melody Myatt? Not Lydia? Surely you don't mean Lady Caroline."

"No, Betty. Sally Bonson."

"No. Not that nice old lady, surely, Abigail dear."

"Betty, what would you do if someone had killed your granddaughter?"

"I would hope that they were arrested and put in prison. But failing that, I would smash them in the face with a mallet. But are you really sure?"

"Okay. Means - When she arrived at the farm, I heard her say to Harvey that she was going to put up the porch awning. So she knew where there was rope, tent pegs, and a mallet.

Motive - She obviously was deeply affected by Cheryl's death. She asked Harvey to get involved in the fun run because the children's ward had looked after her until her death. She even thought it was worth it, knowing how much her mean husband would complain. I think she might have seen Walker somewhere and heard he had something to do with the fun run. Or maybe Verity suggested that she might like to help out. Totally innocently, because I don't think she knew who he was before Ralph told her.

Harvey told Verity in the pub that Sally didn't know anything about what they were up to. But I bet he was always on his phone, and I reckon Harvey can't whisper if he tried. Of course, she heard him. Wives know what their husbands are up to. Especially if it's up to no good. Betty said she had a photo of a young girl by her bed. Not her son, but Cheryl. She had a motive, alright. She loved and missed her granddaughter desperately.

Opportunity - Well, for a start, her van was by the barn. She could have gone at any point when Harvey was busy with the meat, and banged in the tent pegs ready. Caroline said they were there earlier, so it was her plan all along. I expect she said to Sebastian that she had heard a rumour that it wasn't his real name, and would he meet her or something, but when everyone else was asleep. I remember you said she had sleeping pills on her bedside table. She might have slipped two to Harvey. Mind you, I should imagine he was the type that slept like a log anyway. Sally knew she wouldn't be a match for him so she needed to get the upper hand. A tripwire would work perfectly. I wonder if she told him, 'This is for Cheryl,' as she bashed his brains in. Takes a lot of anger to do that. I'm not sure if she knew that Ralph intended to kidnap him to find out where you were buried, Bones. Maybe she did, and she didn't care. It was more important that she had her retribution. She's waited a long time, and I don't think she had much to live for. She spent money on designer clothes, but that meant nothing to her. She probably did it to annoy her skinflint husband. I would have done."

Everyone had gone very quiet. They didn't know whether to feel sorry for the killer or be in shock at how hard the death of her only grandchild had made her, turning her into a vicious killer.

"Do you think she'll confess, hun?"

"I think she thought she was being very clever using the three implements for the killing, knowing everyone would have them. But I don't think she'd want anyone to get in trouble for what she's done. I think that is how we'll get her."

"I'll go to see her tomorrow, on my own, if you don't mind."

"Poor Sally," Betty said for the last time.

Chapter 24

Hayley knocked on the door of the Bonsons' large but decrepit house in Pottlesham. She had waited outside in her Mini until she had seen Harvey pull out of the drive. Probably for his evening drink at the Greyhound pub, she thought. Even sitting outside, she could feel the sadness that was held within the creeper-covered walls, keeping ghosts and emotions from ever leaving.

Sally didn't seem surprised to see Hayley Bennett standing there, and she invited her into the cold, unwelcoming sitting room. Hayley saw a dark aura around the elderly lady that worried her.

"I expect you're surprised at me turning up like this, Mrs Bonson."

"Sally, please. Not at all. In a kind of way, I expected it."

"Can I ask why?"

"I'm a lifetime member of the Women's Institute. I was there when you did a talk for us at Becklesfield Town Hall. There's not a lot that you don't know, and I saw you at the fun run. I believe you call yourself a psychic medium."

"That's right."

"And you've been known to help the police. So no, I'm not surprised. I'm not happy about it. To be honest, I was hoping I would get away with it. I was planning on emptying our bank account and leaving Harvey. I've been looking at some nice hotels in Italy. We had the love of Cheryl in common at one point. He was a completely different man when she was staying with us, which was often, as we looked after her when my daughter-in-law was at work. She was the apple of his eye. She could do and have anything she liked, especially when she was little. This is her when she was five. We had a big party for her here. We hired a magician and a bouncy castle, which cost us a fortune. But that didn't matter. Even Harvey was generous with her. As she got to her teenage years, she was a bit of a handful for our son and his wife, and went off the rails a bit. But she wasn't like that with us. She loved us dearly and was never cheeky or badly behaved while she was here. This is her when we took her on holiday to the seaside." She showed Hayley a photograph of Cheryl sitting on a beach, with her grandad's arm around her.

"Then one night my son phoned. Cheryl had been with friends and taken drugs, and she'd been rushed to Gorebridge hospital. She never woke up, so we couldn't even say goodbye. Have you got children? Can you imagine what it was like for us to see our beautiful Cherry, as we called her, lying there with all those tubes in her?"

"No, Sally. It must have been awful."

"I'll never forget it. I didn't know then that her friend, Louise, had died. I'd met her boyfriend, Elliot, a lovely young lad. I knew he wouldn't have had anything to do with it. But I did wonder after he vanished that night."

"He's dead too, Sally. That's how we know everything. We even know where he's buried."

"Good. His mother deserves that."

"How did you find out that Sebastian was Frank Walker?"

"Harvey, of course. I could hear him talking to a woman from time to time after he'd agreed to do some fundraising for the hospital for me. I had stayed in touch with Verity because we both lost someone we loved, and it was her idea for us to do something for the place where Cherry died. He'd get these calls and take his phone in his room or outside. I know he's my husband, but I couldn't believe that some other woman had romantic designs on him, so I wanted to know what was going on. He's got a voice like a foghorn, so I soon got the gist. He was going to talk to Sebastian on the day after the fun run and not even let me be part of it. I knew everything about the case at the time. Walker was questioned but then let go. He had an alibi from friends, but he could easily have threatened them. Verity and I both thought he was guilty. Actually, I hired a private detective to look into him, and he said he was a drug dealer and he'd been arrested for grievous bodily harm. But he found out that Walker had falsified his alibi and left the country. I was just waiting for him to show his face again. I wanted him dead and planned it so many times as I lay in bed. I hadn't thought of a mallet, but that did the job nicely. Luckily, we had two. We forgot it one year and had to buy another one. That was so lucky when the police checked. I knew I could never lay her to rest till then. And I could never forgive him, even if he was in prison. Can you understand that, Hayley?"

"It's a high price to pay though. You might spend the rest of your life in prison yourself. Especially as by putting in the tent pegs, you made it a premeditated murder. If you hadn't done that, you could have said it was a crime of passion."

"It still was a crime of passion. I could say I had been sent mad by Cherry's death. In a way, that's true. I changed the day she died."

"So what happened on Saturday? How did you get him to meet you?"

"I had to wait till he was on his own, and that wasn't easy. But in the end, I caught him by the barn. I was very honest with him. I simply said that I was the grandmother of a girl he'd given his drugs to, and I needed to talk. He said he had never heard of a Cheryl. And that made me even more angry. She was nothing to him. I didn't tell him my surname in case he mentioned it to Harvey. He had no idea who I was. We were talking by the barn door, and that's when I got the idea. So when no one was about, I pushed in the tent pegs. I'd told him to meet me at midnight, and he did. Luckily, there was no one about. If there had been, I would have done it another time. I'd already put one of my tablets in Harvey's drink, so he didn't hear me leave. But I have no fear of prison. No Harvey to drive me up the wall, and at least it'll be warmer than this old mausoleum."

"Harvey will find it hard without you. I get the sense he loves you very much."

"I know he does. I never doubted that at all. Another reason that I knew he wasn't seeing another woman. But he may have lost me anyway. Hayley, I haven't told anyone this, but I'm ill. It could be weeks or months. But I hope it's not too long. I want to be with Cheryl. Do you think that's possible after what I've done?"

"I'm not sure, Sally. But God is forgiving and knows your reason. I'd like to think that you'll be with her one day. If you really believe in your heart and soul that you had just cause and that you'll see her again, that might be enough. The mind and spirit is strong, even in death."

"Thank you, that's made me feel better. Will you be ringing the police?"

"No. I think it will be better if you give yourself in. I promise I won't tell a living soul. And we don't want anyone else to be arrested. Did you know that Johnson is already suspicious of Lydia?"

"I would never let that happen. Tell me, Hayley, who did kill Penelope? I swear on my life that it wasn't me."

"That's another reason that I think you'll find redemption in death - it was Sebastian March."

Chapter 25

THREE DAYS LATER, JOHNSON WAS GIVING A PRESS conference about the arrest of Sally Bonson. It had been due to him and his team's prompt work in identifying Sebastian March as the drug dealer, Francis Walker. And of course, it had been his own deductions that the suspect had killed him for being responsible for the death of her granddaughter, Cheryl Bonson. Investigations were ongoing to see if he had been responsible for any other deaths.

Johnson wasn't going to mention that PC Tom Bennett had a theory about him having killed Penelope and some boy who had been buried alive at a castle. He'd look into it at a later date, and then take the credit once he knew he was right. The daft lad wanted him to take a chunk out of their budget to dig up the body. That was ridiculous. How could he possibly know where the body was? Unless... no. He wasn't going to fall for her rubbish again. But all the same, he might get Mills to make a few discreet enquiries. To solve a cold case might be a feather in his cap with the Chief Constable. He wouldn't mention that witch, though.

That witch was doing something very important as the press

conference was going on. Hayley had met Ralph Thornton and his mother, Cathy, in the car park at Courtridge Hotel & Spa. Together they walked down the path to the bench where Elliot stood, waiting to see his family for the first time in twelve years. Mother and brother carried bouquets and laid them in front of the bench. Hayley said they should sit while she told them what he was saying.

"Elliot has just said that his memory came flooding back as soon as he saw you both together. He was so worried that he wouldn't know you. All his memories returned, like the time you both took the train to London when you went to the zoo. Every Christmas when you put the decorations up on December the first, and had three artificial trees in the kitchen, sitting room and dining room. Walking him to school in the snow, and watching football with Ralph with their scarves, and keeping warm with a flask of Bovril that you'd made for them. He said you knitted his scarf, Mum, is that right?"

"I did. I still keep it next to my bed," and she started to cry. "Did he suffer at the end?"

Elliot told a white lie. "He says he didn't. He was knocked out and died straight away. He can't remember anything about that night. And when he came to, he was by this lovely lake with no idea how he got here. It's his own piece of paradise, he says. He says he's been happy all these years and only sorry that you had to suffer."

Elliot took his mother's hand, and although the touch was cold, she felt a warm feeling spread through her body.

Ralph said, "We knew he must have been dead. He would have come home else. He was always a good boy for his mum. Such a waste. I wish I had been the one to kill that man."

His mum said, "I'm glad you didn't. I couldn't bear to lose another son. He wasn't worth spending your life behind bars. I feel for Sally Bonson. But I'm a bit jealous all the same. It must have been a nice feeling, for a second at least. She'll find it hard from now on, and it didn't bring Cheryl back."

"I have talked to her. I think she will be alright. She did what she did, and she's not sorry. Elliot said that you should start playing music again, Ralph. He'd forgotten how good you were."

"I'm going to write some new stuff, but from home. Mum's moving in with me in Cornwall. She wouldn't move before, in case you came home. But now she will."

His mother looked shocked, "But what about Elliot? I've got to be near here and put flowers on his resting place."

Hayley couldn't wait to reassure her. "Please don't worry about that. I may be able to get the police to exhume Elliot now. In any case, the owner said she will have her men dig here, and then you can have a proper funeral or cremation. You could have it here or in Cornwall."

"Good idea. I fancy a trip to the west country," Elliot joked. "But can you tell them that it won't be worth coming back here because I won't be here. I've spent enough time at the castle. I'm moving on. Mum, you told me Dad died in the army when I was small," Hayley told her.

"That's right, Lance Corporal Matthew Thornton. There's never been a braver man."

"I see him, Mum. I can see him. In his uniform. He's waving to me."

Cathy only managed to gasp before the tears rolled down her cheeks. "You go, son. Tell your daddy I love him and miss him, and we'll be together again one day."

Elliot squeezed Ralph's shoulder and kissed his mother's cheek. Then Hayley saw him raise his hand and smile to someone that he alone could see.

"He's gone. Elliot has passed on."

Chapter 26

A YOUNG MOTHER WAS PUSHING HER YOUNG SON, Jasper, in his pushchair into Little Chortle to see his Nanny and Grandad. She was going to leave him there and get the bus into Gorebridge to buy a new outfit for a wedding. He was such a cheerful little soul who had a smile for everyone he passed. Even now, he was giggling to himself. She stopped to look at him.

"What are you laughing at, sweetie? Oh, you're so cute."

He pointed and started to babble in his own way.

"It's just a bit of paper blowing in the wind. There's no one there." But his mum did find it a bit strange that a piece of card was just hovering in front of them. She went to grab it, but it jerked out of the way.

"Come on, let's go. That's weird."

Jasper waved at a lady in a nurse's uniform and a young girl. "Bye bye."

"Bye bye," said Suzie. "He's so cute, Lillian."

"He sure is. I was just thinking, though. We didn't think this through. When we get to Anya's house, we can pass through the doors, but Hayley's business card can't."

"I know, I'll put it through the letterbox."

Anya was at school, so when her mother, Anne, heard something drop in the hall, she ran, hoping it was a letter from him. But it was just a card - *The Deadly Detective Agency*. All problems great and small. Paranormal and normal. Well, she had a problem. If only she had a sign that she should use them. A cold breeze came into the hall, but she felt a light touch on the hand that held the card. That was enough for Anne. She picked up her phone and emailed *The Deadly Detective Agency*.

Hayley sat in her car at the hotel. She was taking a few minutes to herself after being with the grieving relatives. It had affected her more than she had thought. An email had come through from someone called Anne. She was desperate. She needed help. She had given her address as Chortle, opposite the Royal Oak pub. She reversed the car and set off to see what she could do for the unhappy woman. She knew at once who this was - Anya's mother.

Lillian and Suzie sat with Anne on the sofa, where she picked up a letter from a pile.

"What does it say?" asked Suzie. "What's that long number at the top?"

"874929. H14. It reminds me of when I worked in A and E. I saw this more than a few times. I think I am beginning to understand. Anya's father isn't dead. He's in prison."

"But why wouldn't she just tell Camille?"

"Embarrassment, shame. And it would depend on what he was in prison for. It could be anything: embezzlement, theft."

"It could be murder. How awful for the family. And there was nothing they could do. I bet Anya misses him like he's dead."

"I expect the social services are already aware of Anya if her dad's in jail."

"My mum and dad got divorced, and that was bad enough. At least I could see him every other week."

"They're allowed to visit," said Lillian.

"For about an hour, I bet."

"Well, he did break the law, Suzie."

"I know, but they didn't. They're being punished too."

"Well, maybe he should have thought of that before he did whatever he did."

Suzie felt a bit of anger towards Lillian for the first time. She saw the crime through the eyes of a child. Anya's daddy was ripped away from her. And for how long? No wonder Anya was shy and didn't want to mix with other children. Thank goodness she had Camille as a friend; she wasn't the sort to judge anyone. But she still hadn't trusted her with the secret. The doorbell rang. Thank goodness, Hayley had arrived.

Hayley nodded at the two spirits, who told her as quickly as they could that Anne's husband was in prison and his name was Grant Finn.

Hayley extended her hand and said, "My name is Hayley. My friends in the agency are very discreet, Anne."

"Sit down, please. I know it said paranormal or normal, but mine is just normal."

"But thankfully for you, I'm not. I can already tell that you need my help. Your husband, I believe, is Grant. And he's had to go away, leaving you and your daughter devastated. You had to move here from your large house. Anya had to leave her private school."

"That's amazing. How on earth can you know all that?"

"And, Anne, I know. He was convicted of murder."

Anne burst into tears, and a shocked Suzie put an arm around her. "He didn't do it. I swear on my life. He was the most gentle man in the world. He wouldn't hurt a fly, or wasp, or even a spider. I promise you. He gave her a lift, that's all."

"Why don't you tell me the whole story, hun."

Chapter 27

A meeting was hurriedly arranged at Hayley's house in Church Lane. Suzie had run to the library and told the others the news. They had a new case!

Betty was delighted. "Come on, Hayley, don't keep us in suspenders."

"We're talking about a case that's two years old, so it's not going to be easy."

"We've just solved one that was twelve years ago, so we can do it. We must do it," said Suzie. "For Anya's sake."

Lillian said, "You have to keep in mind that he might be guilty, sweetheart. There's nothing we can do then."

"I don't think he did. You don't either, do you, Hayley?"

"I'm not sure, hun. But I know Anne doesn't believe he did it, and that's good enough for me, for now. And she's a client, so we owe it to her to look into it.

I'll give you some background to the case. Anne, Grant and Anya Finn lived in Gladstone Forge. A very posh area near Gorebridge. Anne didn't need to work, and Anya went to a private school as a day girl. Grant was an accountant in London, and got the train every day and drove home from the station. This particular evening, two years ago, it was getting dark and raining, and he saw a girl at a bus stop. Obviously getting wet and on her own. He thought of his own daughter and reversed back and offered her a lift. The girl probably thought he looked well-off, so she got in. She said she was going to Bulbury Cross, and he said it was on his way. Her name was Cindy Doyle. She was fourteen years old. They chatted on the way, and he asked her where she went to school, and he told her about Anya. It was all very friendly. Then he dropped her in her village, she thanked him, and that was that.

The next thing they knew, early the next morning, there was an extremely loud knock at the door, and he was taken in for questioning. Apparently, the young girl was found a few minutes' walk from where Grant had dropped her; strangled and laid out on a gravestone."

"I remember it," said Betty. "It was all over the major papers. We can look it up in the library."

"Definitely, hun. And they had CCTV near where Grant had picked her up from. So they had his number plate and her getting in the car willingly. The next thing is, Cindy turns up dead."

"They must have had some other proof," said Abigail. "What was she strangled with?"

"Bare hands, that matched his pretty much. And they could tell by the pressure used to break the hyoid bone that the killer was right-handed like him."

"But that could mean most men."

"And neither wore a wedding ring."

"Plenty of men don't wear wedding rings. My John never did."

"There must have been something else," said Terry.

"Anne said that this was a complete coincidence, but Grant knew the poor girl's mother. He had been engaged to her years ago, and she had broken off the engagement. There was no way he knew that it was her daughter."

"What idiot would think that was a motive?" asked Abigail.

"Er, I bet you can all guess."

"Johnson," they all said.

"Correct. They had DNA and unfortunately for Grant, she had hugged him before she got out and told him how grateful she was. She said she'd been getting really scared as usually she was with friends. So there were even fair hairs on his suit jacket. In no time at all, Anne said he was tried, convicted, and sentenced to life in prison.

She couldn't pay the mortgage after all the legal fees, so they moved to that small house in Chortle. Anya was allowed to stay at the private school till the end of that year and then she moved to a state school. And you know the rest."

"So what can we do? We've got to do something," pleaded Suzie.

"I don't want to yet, but I could ask Tom. I think we need to find out more before we get him in trouble for sharing files."

"Me and Lillian could look at the papers in the library as soon as it closes."

"Good idea, Suzie. Me, Abigail, and Betty could have a drive out to Bulbury Cross. There might be someone there who can tell us about the murder. Nothing happens that locals in a small village don't know. Maybe the vicar will be there as well. Hopefully, it's the same one as back then. I'll take some flowers with us to show Cindy that she's not forgotten and we're going to get justice for her."

"I hate to say it, but she might already have got justice. Just because we feel sorry for his family, it doesn't mean he's innocent. There are lots of wives that don't think their husband could be a killer. Or vice versa. Do you think Harvey Bonson would ever think that his upstanding wife could ever bash someone's brains in?" said Lillian.

"You have a point. But I don't feel it," said Hayley.

"If it's okay with you all, I'd like to go and see Celia Hanson at the *Chiltern Weekly*. I haven't seen her for a while. I think she would have been at the inquest and the trial," said Terry.

"Perfect. Do you want me to drop you off on our way to Bulbury Cross?"

"No thanks. I'll get the bus. Number eight, on the hour, from outside the Post Office."

Hayley, Abigail, and Betty pulled up outside the Roebuck Inn. They decided to get a feel for the area and had a walk around. The village was similar to Becklesfield, but a lot smaller. The whole of Bulbury Cross was on one road. The cross was a stone one that had been built to honour the war dead from as long ago as 1814. Behind this was St Peter's Church, where Cindy's body had been found.

"Anne told me that she had been laid out on the grave of a young girl, Patricia Burnett."

They found her headstone eventually. There were hundreds of bodies that had been buried there over the years and a smaller section for those who had been cremated.

Patricia had one of the more expensive headstones. There was a stone angel looking down on her, and the words — *Treasures in Heaven engraved on it.*

"So sad, bless her little soul," said Hayley. "Born 1939 and died 1942. She was only three."

"No one should outlive their child, or even grandchild. At least I didn't have to suffer that. I had a long, happy life and I wouldn't change a thing."

Abigail said, "I wished I would have had kids, but when I see things like that, or we look into a child's death, I'm quite glad I didn't."

"Me too. These flowers can be for both of them," said Hayley, as she placed them carefully on the overgrown grave.

The vicar came out of the church to see an odd-looking, hippy lady laying down a bouquet of flowers and talking to herself. Not unusual, of course; she must be praying or talking to the departed. "Are you alright there? Anything I can do to help? I'm Nigel, the vicar."

"I'm just looking around. This one is so sad. She was only a baby when she died."

"There's an awful lot of children buried here, I'm afraid. At the beginning of the last century, mothers had anything up to ten children. The death rate was so high that it was the only way of making sure that you had someone to carry on the family name. That's without the women that died in childbirth. Hard times, as Dickens said."

"Then I heard there was a young girl murdered here."

"I don't know if she was murdered here. But she was certainly placed here. In fact, I was the one that found the body. I was locking up the church for the night and I walked through here to get to the rectory. Whether it was God telling me to, but I stopped and looked in this direction and saw her blonde hair. I thought it must be an animal to start with. But as I got closer, I realised. I called the police and they came very quickly."

"What time was it?"

"About seven-thirty. Why are you so interested? I hope you're not a journalist or one of those true crime bloggers. We've had them all here."

"Actually, I'm a friend of the family trying to make some sense of it."

"I thought I'd met all the friends and family of Cindy. I don't remember you from the funeral."

"Ah, sorry, not Cindy's family. Grant Finn's family."

"That's different; I don't think I should say any more. But I have said a prayer for them."

"Did you know him?"

"Not at all. He didn't come to church here. I think he had a big house in the country."

"Do the Doyles still live here?"

"No, they moved to Hampshire. Too many memories."

"Were they satisfied that the right man had been caught?"

"They had no doubt at all. None of us did. Maybe before the court case. But there was too much evidence. The inspector was very convincing in his statement. Now what was his name? A bit of an uncouth man. Jackson, I think."

"Johnson," said Hayley, with a sigh.

"That's the one. They're not thinking of opening the case again, are they? That would make for a lot of bad feelings and publicity that we certainly don't need."

"The police aren't, but someone is. Thank you, Reverend, for your help."

As he walked away, he looked back and saw her talking to herself again. He decided he ought to do something. Yes, he'd phone Mrs Doyle; she should know if it was all going to be in the papers again.

Hayley went to the pub and forgot she was on her own until all the locals stopped talking and looked round. She got so used to talking to Abigail and Betty that she forgot she was the only one that could see them.

"What can I get you, miss?" said the middle-aged man behind the bar.

"Hmm, just an orange juice, please?"

"Haven't seen you here before."

"I just took some flowers to your beautiful churchyard. For Cindy Doyle."

"That was a terrible tragedy. No one could believe that could happen here. Are you friends of theirs?"

"No, I've never met them. But I know someone who thinks that they might have the wrong man."

A look of anger replaced the friendly face. "We were there when he was sent down. Whoever told you that is way off, so forget it. You better have your drink and leave." Once again the pub went silent and all eyes were on the stranger. No one wanted to make eye contact with Hayley, and leaving her drink, she left the pub. It was then that she saw the old, silent man for the first time.

At just about that same time, Terry was at the offices of the *Chiltern Weekly*. He had found the deceased journalist, Celia Hanson, looking over the shoulder of a fellow newswriter.

"Hello, Terry. No Abigail today? That's not like her to miss out on something."

"No, she let me come all on my own."

"How are things going between the pair of you? I hear you're getting all loved-up."

"Don't tell her I said so, but I love the bones of her, if you'll excuse the pun," he said with a smile. "She drives me crazy when I'm with her, and I miss her when she's not there. And she's big-headed enough as it is, so I can hardly tell her that I think she's beautiful, clever, and just perfect."

"You should. Us women often act confident but underneath we're all a bit vulnerable at heart."

"Even Abigail?"

"Especially Abigail. Someone actually took her life. She's probably very fragile under that bossiness and confidence."

"It must be a long way under. Do you really think so?" asked Terry.

"I do. So make sure you tell her exactly how you feel. So what can I do for you? Now I've given you advice from the 'Dear Celia' section of the *Chiltern Weekly*."

"The agency has got another client. Her name is Anne Finn, and her husband is sitting in a prison cell convicted of the murder of a young girl. She said he's innocent. It was a couple of years ago. His name is Grant Finn, and the girl he killed was Cindy Doyle."

Celia nodded. "You don't need a photographic memory to remember that case. I know it well. I was already dead, but I still went to the inquest and trial for the paper. It's a shame, I would have written a very good piece. She was fourteen and found at the church in Bulbury Cross."

"That's the one. We heard he was found guilty because he gave the girl a lift home, just trying to be kind. And he knew the girl's mother from years before. How they found him guilty, I'll never know."

"There was a lot more evidence than that, Terry. Didn't Anne tell you?"

"No, she didn't."

"For one thing, they proved he had a temper. And I bet you didn't know that a social worker had been called to look into his young daughter." Celia closed her eyes. "Her name was Anya. And this might help you; the social worker was Sonia, Suzie's mother. Apparently, she'd been taken to the hospital with a broken ulna, lower arm. This was the year before the murder. They thought it might be a defensive wound. At the trial, the school said they had concerns in the past over bruises. Her PE teacher gave evidence at the trial for the prosecution."

"We didn't know. We just assumed that he was a family man and innocent. Suzie and Lillian did say she was as quiet as a mouse, maybe that's why. But his wife is convinced he couldn't have done it. What about timing? Did he have time?"

"Hang on, I'll need to think about that one. Hmm, he gave her a lift at five-twenty. That was caught on the CCTV. And Bulbury Cross was about fifteen minutes away, so five-thirty-five. And another ten minutes till he got home. So he should have been home just before six. The housekeeper swore in court that he walked in the door at half past. The body was found at about half seven. Grant Finn said he'd pulled in the drive and sat there for half an hour before he went in. He said he'd had a hard day and wanted to chill out on his own in the car."

"I can believe that."

"But unfortunately, the jury couldn't, Terry. They saw him as a child abuser and murderer with a temper. DNA put the final nail in his coffin. Guilty as charged. Life without parole."

"That's not going to please Hayley. She always sees the good in people."

"But, and this is only a little but, there was something strange though. Johnson wouldn't have even thought of it, but with my eidetic memory I did connect another case. I can sometimes see a pattern when no one else can. This one happened a year before the death of Cindy. And even I didn't see it until now, but there was another murder after her death. If I had been alive, I probably would have."

"Anything I can take back to the others will help."

"The first one was an elderly woman; I think that's why no one thought of it. The last one was a schoolboy of seventeen. So not similar at all. The only connection I see is the Bible quotes. The woman had been to her scriptures class and a passage had been circled in her open Bible. And, now I think of it, the boy had a bookmark in his rucksack. His mother said she'd never seen it before. On it was a quote. I'm sure it will be on the crime scene photos in the respective files. Maybe Tom Bennett can get them for you. I saw them at the inquests but didn't actually read them. Both of the MOs were different. One was death by a blunt instrument, and the boy was stabbed. The lady was found on the verge of the lane that ran past the church, and the boy was hidden under a big pile of leaves. No one has been arrested so far. Just another two unsolved murders. If your detective agency had been going when the girl was killed, I could have told you my suspicions."

"We'll look into it now, don't worry. I don't suppose you know the names of the victims, do you?"

"Let me see. Er, Beryl Carstairs killed in Lower Abslow, and George Buttler in Great Heron."

"You're a lifesaver, Celia. We'll make sure you get the credit for this if it all comes out."

"Good luck with that. You know who the SO was, don't you?"

"Yes, our own Johnson, and that's an added bonus when we prove him wrong. And Finn was already banged up when the last murder took place."

"Now don't forget to make a fuss of Abigail. She's good for you, Terry. Before she came along, you were wandering about Becklesfield like a lost soul. She's certainly added excitement to your life. And love."

"And she's got a heart of gold underneath all that armour and brashness."

"So let me know if there's anything more I can do for you with the case. If anything else occurs to me, I'll come to the library. Goodness knows how I'll get there."

"The number eight bus, half past the hour, from the bus station!"

Chapter 28

TERRY NEARLY MISSED THE MEETING AT THE LIBRARY and arrived as Hayley was going through what they had found out in Bulbury Cross.

"So basically, no one in the Roebuck Inn would talk to me after that. Clammed up like a, well, clam, I suppose. But I did learn from the vicar, Nigel, that everyone thought Finn was guilty. I don't think they would want to think that it was anyone local. Even if there wasn't a lot of evidence."

Terry joined them and said, "Actually, there was quite a lot of evidence. I don't think that Anne was totally honest with you, Hayley. I suppose she wanted you to take the case pretty badly. There were two things: Anya had been taken to hospital and had a broken arm and some bruises. And on the night Cindy Doyle was murdered, there was about half an hour that Grant couldn't account for. He says he was sitting outside his posh house in his car before he went in."

"Could be true," said Betty. "John did that sometimes when the kids were young. After a day at work, he sometimes unwound before he had the family chaos to deal with."

"Doesn't look good though, does it?" said Abigail. "Especially if he hurt Anya."

Suzie bristled. "I don't believe that at all. If that was the case, she'd be glad he wasn't there anymore. And her mum wouldn't have phoned you if he was violent."

"Calm down, Suzie, I haven't finished. That's the bad news. There might be some good news for Anne and Anya. Hayley, when you went to where they found Cindy Doyle, did you see a Bible quote at the crime scene anywhere?"

"We did. It was on the grave of the little girl. It said 'Treasures in Heaven,' I think. Why?"

"Well, Celia can remember two other murders which had verses from the Bible at the scene. Not there, but not that far away. One was before, and one was after. She thought, looking back, it might have been done by the same person."

"There's a lot of God-fearing folk around here, so it could be a coincidence. But Celia is very good at finding the common denominator."

Betty sighed and shook her head. "You can't call them common, Abigail."

"I didn't call anyone common, Betty."

"Yes, you did, a denominator. As you know, my John was into that kind of thing, and I often dressed up as one. I had a particularly tight, black…"

"I just meant that Celia is very good at seeing links between things. So we need to look into them as well. Where were the murders, Terry?"

"Beryl Carstairs, aged 56, was bludgeoned in Lower Abslow, and George Buttler, who was only seventeen, was stabbed in Great Heron."

"So no wonder they weren't connected, what with the different sexes, ages and MOs. Serial killers usually go for the same type. Tom won't be pleased, but I'll have to get him to take a peek at the files. But it's a start. Once we get more details, if it looks like there is a connection, I'll go and see Reverend Pete, and he can tell me the context of the verses and where they're from. Before I go, Terry, could I have a word with you?"

"Of course, anything for you, Hayley."

"Is there a new Dead around? An elderly man, not a murder, I don't think. He's definitely trying to get my attention. He was outside the Roebuck Inn, and I swear, I nearly ran him over as I pulled away. Then I saw him outside the library."

"I can't say I've seen him. But they come and go, especially at that age. What did he look like?"

"Short, grey hair, brushed forward. Burgundy V-neck jumper, shirt and tie, and brown trousers. He didn't say anything or look distressed, just looked at me for a few seconds and then went. But the funny thing is, he told me his name is Benjamin. He didn't move his lips, just told me silently somehow."

"Benjamin? I'll go and check around the church now. He'll be there if he's anywhere."

"Thank you, Terry. I'm not even going to mention it to Tom. He's already going to be annoyed he's got to look up those other cases."

Tom was indeed annoyed that he had to look up more case files. DCI Johnson had him walking around the back streets of Gorebridge when he found out that he had a hand in getting Sally Bonson arrested. Tom had only had one break and now he had to spend it looking up cold cases. And Hayley didn't even know the dates. He had the victims' names and that was all.

He took as many photographs on his phone as he could, and nearly got caught when Dave Mills came into the room. But luck was on his side, and he sent the evidence to Hayley immediately. He hoped she had got it, as he deleted everything as soon as he could. She'd get him sacked in the end!

Abigail was already at Hayley's house, so they went through the information together.

"So Beryl Carstairs was a church elder. Even more connection to the church then. Which church is that?" asked Abigail.

"St John's, Lower Abslow. She'd been to Bible reading class and was found in the lane, just past the churchyard. Blunt force trauma to the back of the head. The weapon was something like a pipe maybe.

Then the young boy, George Buttler, God bless him, was stabbed in the back with a nine-inch kitchen knife. That was in Great Heron. He was found under a large pile of leaves, not far from the church. But it is a small village, so that might not be relevant. Here's the bookmark. It says, 'No one can serve two masters.' Is that to do with school, or two gangs even?"

"It doesn't mention drugs or gangs, does it?"

"And on the grave where Cindy was, it said, 'Treasures in Heaven.' That must be because the little one was in Heaven. I can't think what there could be in common, but we've got nothing else, hun. And here's a photo of the one in the woman's Bible. 'The power of the wicked will be broken.' It's too late to go and see Pete tonight, but we'll pop by the church tomorrow. Do you fancy coming?"

"Always. Not like I've got anything else to do."

"I thought you were going to the seaside with Terry."

"I know, but he hasn't mentioned it again, and the agency keeps getting in the way. We could do with some time together."

"I could give you both a lift, hun."

"Terry seems to think it will be more fun to go by train. I can't say I thought it was much fun when I was alive. All those people packed in one space."

"He probably means romantic. Don't forget he's from the era with that love film and the train."

"What film's that? Don't think I saw it."

"It was an old black-and-white one. They were having an affair and they split up at the train station."

"Doesn't sound very romantic to me. Especially if they split up."

"You probably have to see it. What was the name of it now? It had Trevor Howard in it."

"Never heard of him. I'm obviously far too young."

"I'm younger than you. I saw it with Tom's parents one Christmas. I think it was called 'Close Encounter.'"

"I thought that was spaceships, not trains."

"No, hun, it was definitely trains. Hang on, hun. Don't look now, but can you see that man behind you?"

"Not if I can't look."

"Okay, look."

Abigail turned her head slowly. "By the window?"

"Yes."

"No, I can't. I honestly can't, Hayley."

"I can see him as plain as day. He's gone now. Am I going crazy?"

"Probably, but don't worry about it. I believe you. He must have something to say just to you."

"Maybe. So far the only thing I know is that he's called Benjamin. I'm going to lie down on the sofa, I've been feeling a bit strange lately. I think it's something to do with my gift. I've been feeling all these empathic feelings I've never had before."

"You rest, Hayley. I'll come back about ten in the morning, and we'll go and see Reverend Pete. Just shows, once we've solved this one, we should all take a break."

Chapter 29

Hayley had only just finished her bowl of cereal before Abigail burst through her wall. She had been followed by Tiggy, Luna's mother, so for once Luna didn't mind being left on her own. As long as she was fed first, of course.

Hayley had written the details in her pad. There was a lot to remember, what with the Bible passages and different villages. And her memory had been hopeless lately.

Pete's wife, Mary, answered the door at the vicarage and showed Hayley into the study, where Pete was writing a report to the Bishop. She said she would make them both a coffee and left them to it. Abigail thought Pete looked very handsome in his clerical collar and a black V-neck jumper; rather like the one in *Grantchester* on the telly. No wonder the ladies of the parish all fancied him.

"Sorry to disturb you, Pete. Are you busy?"

"It's coming up to the Harvest Festival, so there's always plenty to do this time of year; with the school concerts and food collections. But I've always got time for you, Hayley."

"Thank you for that. We—well, I should say I—want to pick your brains about the Bible, Pete."

"No pressure then. I'd better be able to, or I've wasted my entire life," he laughed.

"Nothing too complicated, like how water was turned into wine. But if you did know, that would be very handy."

"Wouldn't it just."

"There are three passages that I need to know about. Not particularly what books they're in, but more what they're about."

"Fabulous. I always like my parishioners to get into the Bible. It's the bestselling book of all time, you know?"

"Is it really?"

"Contrary to belief, it's not the one about a wizard. If you are really interested, we have Bible readings in the church hall every Tuesday at two o'clock. Then there are prayer meetings on a Thursday."

"I hate to disappoint you, Pete. I'd love to say I've developed a sudden need to read it, but it's part of my research. You see, I'm writing a book."

"Oh well, worth a try. Hit me."

Hayley got out her pad and pen. "The first one is on a child's gravestone: 'Treasures in Heaven'. Then, 'The power of the wicked will be broken'. And the last one was on a bookmark: 'No one can serve two masters'. Can you see a link between the content?"

Pete nodded and felt rather relieved that he knew all the quotes. "You might as well have said Timothy 6, verse 10: 'For the love of money is the root of all kinds of evil. It is through this craving that some have wandered away from the faith and pierced themselves with many pangs'. They are all about wealth and riches."

"Ah, that is very interesting. I hadn't caught that. So could we go through them, please?"

"The first one is Matthew 6.19: 'Do not store up for yourselves treasures on earth, where moths and vermin destroy, and where thieves break in and steal. But store up for yourselves treasures in Heaven. For where your treasure is, there your heart will be also'."

"That's very beautiful. So it's aimed at a rich person."

"But on the headstone, I suppose the parents just liked the sentiment of their greatest treasure being in Heaven. Now the second one is from Psalm 37: 'Better the little that the righteous have than the wealth of many wicked; for the power of the wicked will be broken'. See, money again."

"And on the bookmark was, 'You cannot serve two masters'."

"That's the easiest and most well-known one. I believe it's Matthew again and quite self-explanatory. The two masters are God and money."

"That's brilliant, Pete. I had every faith in you, if you'll excuse the pun," said Hayley, just as Mary came in with a tray of coffee and jam tarts.

"Here we are. Don't worry, I didn't bake them. Got them from the village shop."

"Thank you. I hope you can join us, Mary," said Hayley.

"No, I'll leave you to it. I'm just off to see Rebecca Jones. We're going shopping in town. See you later, darling."

"I'm so pleased. She was very lonely when she first moved here. And her husband works such long hours."

"Mary is better with lost souls than I am, luckily."

"You're a very lucky man, Pete."

"I know. I thank the Lord every day. Is there anything else you need to know?"

"What do you know about Bulbury Cross, Great Heron, and Lower Abslow?"

"They're quite close to each other. Only thing I can think of is that they're in the same parish—the Diocese of Middle Chiltern."

"What does that mean exactly?"

"The churches in those villages are under the same bishop.

This one is under the Parish of St. Barnaby. There are about nine churches, including this one. I've no idea how many there are in Middle Chiltern. Does that help?"

"Not really. We already knew that the three cases happened close together."

"Whoops," said Abigail.

"Cases? You're not sleuthing again, are you, Hayley?"

"I was hoping to keep it quiet, so don't tell anyone. But a man called Grant Finn was found guilty of killing a young girl, and we think he may be innocent."

"Cindy Doyle. I remember it. And you think he's innocent?"

"Maybe. And there are two other murders that you've just confirmed could be connected. And if they are, that means he's innocent."

"Or he killed twice more," suggested Pete.

"He was in prison for the last one, luckily. So if we're right, that means that there's another murderer on the loose."

"I can't do much to help, Hayley, but I'll pray to keep you safe. There's another verse that you should keep close to your heart and mind: 'And that we may be delivered from wicked and evil men. For not all have faith'. Be careful, please."

Hayley and Abigail left the vicarage happy with the amount they had learned. They knew that Reverend Pete would keep the knowledge to himself. It wasn't like a confessional, but he had very high morals.

"So, Abi, if there is another murderer out there, I think we can agree that he has a problem with rich people, and knows the Bible from cover to cover."

"So a hard-up, religious maniac, or, I hate to say it, a vicar!"

Chapter 30

"So, assuming that our vicar isn't a maniacal murderer, what's the plan?" asked Lillian.

Hayley answered first. "Pete said they're all churches in the same parish. Let me google Middle Chiltern. Hmm, Middle Chiltern is an ancient ecclesiastical parish, created in 1844. It includes Lower Abslow, Bulbury Cross, Parsley Green, Great Heron, Brambly, Dagford and, that's strange, Chortle. Now that is a coincidence; that's where Anne and Anya live. So there are seven altogether."

"We still need to know if there's anything else in common. Like bingo in the church hall. Maybe he doesn't approve of gambling. Or pubs. There's other things in villages."

Betty said, "I've no idea how much a church wedding is these days, but I've heard it's an awful lot of money. John and I got married in St Mary's Church and that cost twenty-five shillings back then."

"That's true, it could be a disgruntled groom."

"Or bride, dear."

"No, hun, because they convicted Grant because of the size of his hands."

"Some women have huge hands, dear."

"Maybe. We'll keep it in mind. But it could be a widower who couldn't afford to have his wife buried in the churchyard. I still think it's to do with the churches. I mean, they were all close to where the bodies were."

Abigail said, "We need to see exactly where they found the bodies. Let's start with the first one. Lower Abslow. Are you coming, Terry?"

"Definitely. What about you, Betty?"

"I'm going with Lillian and Suzie to Anya's house. I haven't met Anne yet. I want to see what kind of person she is."

"That reminds me, I forgot to say, I'm getting terrible these days, but I rang Anne about Anya's bruises, and she did it on roller skates. Apparently, she had some for her birthday and refused to wear the pads and helmet. And Grant could get angry, but she wouldn't say he had a temper. He shouted at a group of kids that were throwing stones at a dog once, that was all. So that puts our minds at rest."

"I didn't believe it for a second," said Suzie.

"Okay, let's go and see what it's like in Lower Abslow. Let's try and speak to the vicar of St John's. I hope he's as nice as our Pete."

Like at Bulbury Cross, the church was a magnificent centrepiece of the village. But there wasn't much else there. Not even a pub, thought Abigail. Straight away they looked for the vicarage and saw a lady with a large hat, weeding in the garden.

"Excuse me, would it be possible to have a word with the vicar?"

"If you don't mind if she carries on gardening," said the lady with short, grey hair and a kind smile.

"Oh, I'm sorry. How sexist of me."

"Happens all the time. At least you didn't say, 'Are you sure?'. Gail Marston," she said, as she took off a flowery glove to shake hands.

"Hayley Moon. I'm writing a book, and I wanted to do a chapter on local churches and crime in this area."

"I wouldn't like to think the two are connected."

"Oh, sorry, I didn't mean it to sound like that. I'll start again. Were you here when a lady called Beryl Carstairs was murdered?"

"Yes, I was. I knew her very well through the church. She did a lot for us and is very much missed at St John's."

"Did they ever find the person who killed her?"

"We're not far from the by-pass here, so it was thought that someone came from elsewhere and it was a totally random killing. She didn't have any enemies. There was no DNA to match or witnesses. It happened about eight o'clock and was as black as pitch that night. She was on her way home from our weekly Bible reading class."

"I heard that there was a passage marked in her Bible, ringed with a pen."

"Was there? I can assure you that's not anything we do, especially Beryl. The Bible isn't to be drawn on."

"Did you know that there've been another two murders in your parish of Middle Chiltern? I've talked to the vicar of Bulbury Cross, and next I'm going to see the vicar of St Agnes, at Great Heron."

"There isn't a resident vicar at Great Heron anymore. Or at Brambly. There are seven churches in our parish, but the Church saw fit to cut two vicars out completely, and the remaining five do their duties between us."

Hayley was shocked. "Really? That's awful. Why would they do that? The church is the centre of all village life."

"Why does anyone do anything these days? Clergy is no different – Money!"

Abigail and Terry grabbed each other, as Hayley tried to keep calm.

"Money? I thought the Church had plenty of money."

"Not as much as they used to, obviously, so they cut where they can these days. But it's particularly hard on a vicar to be suddenly sacked. Neither of them were given new posts. So not only did they lose their jobs and livelihood, they lost their homes. And of course, it had been their vocation all their lives. It wouldn't surprise me if they eventually sell the vicarages for a tidy profit. They're often the best house in the village."

"Did you know them? I was wondering if you knew where they are now?"

"Goodness, this was four years ago. I think the one from Brambly was called, er, Julian Drake, and the one from Great Heron was Martin Smith. It was dreadful for the parishioners as well. Very unsettling. And I'm sure the congregations halved overnight. They tried to get the Bishop to change his mind. They wrote letters, petitions, had meetings, but nothing would change their minds. I guess I was lucky that I'm a woman. They're trying to be more politically correct these days. It could easily have been my church."

"Well, you've given me a lot to think about, Gail. Thank you."

"Good. So will I see you on Sunday morning, Hayley? Ten o'clock?"

"Actually, I live in Becklesfield, so I'm already spoken for," she laughed.

"Pete Steven's church? Give him my regards. A lovely man."

"He is. I can't imagine what we would do if they got rid of him. If not murder, a mutiny. I think even those that don't go to church would fight to keep him. There's so much else a vicar does, isn't there? Thank you again."

Hayley had a job to keep quiet before she got back to the car. "Now we're getting somewhere. The motive of money and two suspects."

"Or even more if you think it could be one of the angry churchgoers," said Terry.

"I've just had an even worse thought," said Abigail. "Seven churches, three murders, right? The murders were done three years ago, then two, when Cindy was killed. And then one year ago. What time of the year were they killed? Do we know?"

Terry said, "I remember Celia saying that George Buttler's body was hidden in a big pile of leaves. So I'm thinking autumn."

"I'll go and ask exactly when Beryl was murdered."

"And ask when the two vicars were let go, Hayley," shouted Abigail after her.

Hayley ran back to the garden, where Gail was pruning a large hydrangea bush. Abigail and Terry saw her running back with a huge smile on her face.

"You were both right, Beryl was killed in the autumn. And she knows exactly when they lost their jobs. She says it was particularly sad, as they had both collected so much for the Harvest Festival. The first week in October!"

Abigail's eyes widened. "Hayley, I think you'd better get in touch with Tom, quick as you can. There are four churches still on that list. Harvest Festival is this Sunday, and I have an awful feeling that there's going to be another murder."

Chapter 31

TOM WAS SURE HE HAD TOLD HAYLEY THAT IT WOULD be the last time that he looked up cold cases, but now he had to go into the database to find the addresses of two ex-vicars. Good job he loved her. If Johnson found out, he would be as sacked as they were. And anyway, vicars didn't go around killing at random. She was definitely wrong this time. But he found the addresses and sent them to Hayley. Afterwards, he insisted that if they were guilty, she should stay well away. But he knew she wouldn't take any notice. She never had before.

So the following morning, Hayley pulled up outside a block of flats on the edge of Gorebridge. She had brought Suzie for protection and also Abigail. Neither of them liked the look of the area, so they insisted that she stay in the car until they checked out the ex-reverend, Martin Smith. Hayley didn't disagree for once and locked the doors of her red Mini.

Abigail and Suzie walked up the stairs to the second floor and into flat twenty-seven. They were disappointed that the man himself wasn't there. They wanted to know if he looked like a crazed serial killer, even though most of the killers they had met looked quite normal. It didn't look like the lair of a madman either. There were no religious words scrawled on walls, or photos of victims marked with a red cross. In fact, it was rather tidy, and it was evident that Martin Smith lived on his own.

"Well, this is a bit disappointing," said Abigail. "He might have left in a hurry. Look, he's left his bowl of cornflakes on the table. No milk, I bet. He'll probably be back in a minute."

"Does that mean he's a cereal killer?" laughed Suzie.

"Hey, I do the funny jokes," smiled Abigail. "But very good. Look at all the photos of him at weddings and christenings. Shows how popular he was. No other photos of a family."

"They probably were his family. Quite sad, actually."

"Doesn't mean he didn't do the murders. Just shows he lost more than a job. He lost the love and adoration of his flock. I can't see a crucifix, or even a bible."

"There's this," shouted Suzie from the bedroom. Above the chest of drawers was a cross-stitch tapestry in a frame. On it, in red and blue, was written, 'Satan disguises himself as the angel of light'.

"Makes a change from 'No place like home', I suppose. Not quite so catchy," said Abigail.

"Sounds a bit scary."

There was a black and white photograph underneath it, of a woman dressed in black and her young son, in which neither of them were smiling. "Now she does look scary. You wouldn't want to bump into her on a dark night. He looks about five there. Must be his mum. Have a look around for any weapons, Suzie."

"I'll check the drawers for a gun or something. Here's a bible, but no weapons." After ten minutes, Suzie admitted defeat, and they went back to the car. From an alley, they saw a scruffy-looking man, carrying a plastic shopping bag, walking towards them. He was thin and had long, grey hair that reached his shoulders and a bushy beard. Hayley recognised him from the files that Tom had sent, so she got out of the car and approached him.

"Excuse me, aren't you Reverend Smith? I used to love listening to your sermons when you were the vicar of Great Heron." Before he could answer, she had grabbed his hand to shake. She held onto it until he snatched it back.

"I was. I don't remember you, though. Now if you will excuse me, I have things to do."

Hayley got back in the car and stayed silent while she processed what she had sensed.

"Are you okay, Hayl? I can tell by your face, you felt something, didn't you?"

"It wasn't good. I saw a place and I saw anger. But I saw darkness in his eyes. He's angry. His thoughts are on one thing only. His thoughts are on murder and revenge. We must get back to the others."

Abigail told them, "We needn't even go to see the other vicar. Martin Smith is the one. Hayley saw it in his eyes. He's going to murder someone in one of the other four villages. I'm sure of it. The Harvest Festival is coming up. But where will it be?"

"And when?" said Terry. "The other ones were before and after. So it could be any time in the next week or two."

"Unless we follow him. The other murders were early evenings, so we needn't be there all day," said Lillian. "Suzie and I could do that."

"That would be brilliant, hun. I couldn't get close again, not now he's seen me."

"It would be too dangerous anyway. We've already nearly lost you once," said Betty.

"I might even be able to phone the police if we know for sure he's going to murder someone else. Although I've never tried before," said Suzie.

"But they wouldn't be able to hear you, hun. You'd need to tell me, and I'd ring Tom."

"As long as you don't go anywhere near him," said Abigail. "So at least we have a plan. Tonight and for the next few nights, Suzie and one of us will go to the flat and watch Martin Smith. You'd better start tonight. I wish we knew where it was going to be. But we'll be ready for him. I'd stake my life on it!"

Just two nights later, Suzie and Lillian watched a strange occurrence. Martin had been increasingly jumpy and had taken to mumbling to himself. He sat at the kitchen table and took a card out of an envelope. It was a thank-you card. He wrote on it, and Lillian immediately knew tonight was the night. They watched as he put on his coat and pulled a black, woollen hat low down on his head. Lastly, he added thick, black gloves, and he was ready. He left the flats and walked quickly through the alley into Gorebridge town centre, with murder on his mind.

He went into the busy shopping centre and went into a few shops, but it wasn't until they all got to the bus station that Lillian and Suzie lost him.

Hayley's phone rang with an unknown number. "Hello."

"Hayley, can you hear me? It's Suzie. I've stolen someone's phone."

"I can hear you. What happened?"

"I'm sorry, we lost him. He must have thought that someone was following him. There were loads of buses, and he kept running around. We have no idea where he was going."

"Don't worry, hun. He might just be visiting someone."

"No. It's going to be tonight. We saw him writing a thank-you card. Something about camels and needles. Lillian thought it had something to do with money again."

"She's right. You're still at the bus station? Okay, I'll pick you both up right away, and we'll take it from there. Bye."

"This is it, Abigail. They lost him, and he's on his way. We need to work out where he's going, and fast. Then I'll ring Tom. He should be finishing soon." Hayley grabbed her keys and her phone, and they headed for the car.

"Are you sure you didn't have any idea where, from when you held his hand?"

"It could have been anywhere, hun. I saw a brief flash. Let me try to recreate it. Um, it was dark. It was quiet. Hang on, I saw a tree by water."

"That's good. What else?"

"Just a tree. Like it was drawn. The perfect tree."

"Was it a pine? Or like one of the ones in Ridgeway Wood?"

"Oh God, I'm not very good with trees. It was one of those big ones. Oh yes, it has acorns, or is it conkers?"

Abigail blew out her cheeks. "Hang on, I'm thinking. What were the villages again?"

"Brambly, Great Heron, Chortle and…"

"Chortle, that's it. There's a pond and if I'm not mistaken, drumroll, what is the name of the pub?"

"You're brilliant, Abi. The Royal Oak!"

·

Chapter 32

THE MAN, WHO WAS ONCE THE REVEREND MARTIN Smith, was hiding behind a large tree on the village green. He was feeling cold and hoped that he wouldn't have to wait too long. He had been lucky the other times. The girl and the boy had walked past more or less straight away. He thought how clever he was not to do a killing in Great Heron first. That would have been a bit obvious. And no one ever did connect the three murders. God was on his side; that was why. He already knew that he was going to kill that Beryl woman. She would still have the Bible in her hand from the meeting. But even then, she had taken ages to leave. Talk, talk, talk. He almost gave up. But thank the Lord, she walked right in front of him.

He was hoping for a woman tonight. A man might be too much for him, even with the power of God. It was just as well he'd stopped in town on the way and bought himself a hammer. "I'm doing it for you, Mother," he whispered. In his other pocket, he felt for the thank-you card that he would put on the body.

It showed that he was the righteous one. The God-fearing avenger. His mother would be so proud, God rest her soul. He was carrying on her good works. Maybe when he'd made his point, he'd target the Bishop. He wouldn't listen to him. He wouldn't listen to his congregation, who loved him. He should pay for his sins like Mother made him pay when he was young.

It was up to him to take revenge on those at the top and stop what was happening to his church. He said aloud, "Those who plough evil and those who sow trouble reap it." His mother had made him repeat it every time he was wicked and then punished.

He'd heard the voice in his head and knew what he had to do. And now it looked like his prayer had been answered. A small car drove along the lane and stopped not far from him. An old-fashioned Mini, and he couldn't believe it when a woman with long, black hair got out and looked around. "Yes, Mother, I see her." Was someone with her? She was talking, but no, she was on her own. Maybe on her phone. He'd better wait till she stopped. She was coming his way and not talking now.

He tightened his hold on the hammer and silently withdrew it from his coat. Three more paces, and she would be right in front of him. Two, one more. She passed him, and he raised his arm to strike.

But he missed. Had someone pushed her out of the way? And the hammer was ripped out of his hand by someone—something. What was happening? Martin Smith didn't have time to react, as he was suddenly face down in the damp grass, and his arms were pinned behind his back and handcuffed. He watched as the card was pulled by an unseen hand from his pocket and laid before him. He shouted out as he got to his feet, "Help me, Lord." He hadn't worked out yet that the Lord had never been on his side; it was the devil.

"What the hell do you think you're doing here, Hayley?" Tom grabbed his wife tight as WPC Jane Nichols walked back to the police car with a shocked Martin Smith. "You're lucky we were in the area on a job."

"You don't know how happy I was to see you. I had no idea he'd be waiting here."

"Come on, and I'll take you home, and you can tell me exactly what has been going on. CID and forensics will be here in a minute, but I don't care what Johnson says; I'm coming with you."

"Honestly, I'm fine. Don't fuss."

"Of course, I'm taking you home. You can't drive."

"No, sorry, Tom. I wasn't talking to you. Abigail and the others are all worried to death, and wondering if I'm okay. Honestly, I am. I just want to get home with Tom. Yes, you can all get in the car, Abigail. Like I could stop you."

Tom looked around as a lady approached and said, "Excuse me, ma'am, this is a crime scene. Please keep back."

"Is that you, Hayley? Is everything okay?"

"Tom, this is Anne Finn; I told you about her. What are you doing here, hun?"

"I'm just posting a letter to Grant. Why? What happened?"

"Oh my God, if you had left a bit earlier, it could have been you. I really need to talk to you, but not now. Go home, Anne, I'll be in touch. I've got some news."

"Good news?" asked Anne.

"The best, but not now. I need to get home and rest."

Tom led Hayley away with his arm firmly around her. "Please do what she says and leave the police to do their job, Mrs Finn. And that applies to you as well, Hayley. Stay out of things. I know what you're going to say: a boat is safe in harbour, but that's not what ships are for. But I wish you'd spring a leak or something, and stay tied up to the dock."

"I nearly did spring a leak when Suzie suddenly pushed me, and I saw the hammer, hun. But seriously, how could I live with myself if her poor daughter had been left on her own? I only came to look, honestly. I had no idea he would attack me. But I'm sorry; from now on, I'll be as good as gold."

"Hmm. Why don't I believe that?"

But rest was the last thing that Hayley got that night. Tom made her lie on the sofa and gave her a hot, sweet cup of tea while he listened to how they found out that Smith was going to kill someone that night. Luna hadn't got off her lap either. He sensed she was troubled. He could smell it and even felt a tremor to her body that wasn't usually there. He would do her a favour and sleep on her pillow tonight instead of the other one.

Then, after Tom had gone back to work to write his report, the other members of The Deadly Detective Agency all began to talk. They hadn't left her side since it had happened.

"Please don't all speak at once. Suzie, first of all, thank you so much for saving my life. I didn't even see the man, let alone the hammer."

"I was so glad I pushed you out of the way. You didn't hurt yourself, did you?"

"Not as much as a hammer would have done. No, I fell on grass, so I'm fine. And you were the one that made the phone call. If you hadn't, Anne would have been the fourth victim for sure."

Abigail put an arm around Hayley. "I've never felt so helpless. I wish you had been there, Terry."

"I wish I was. I thought we told you not to take any more chances, Hayley. You're no good as a medium if you're dead as well. Not to mention that Tom would be as mad as a wet hen."

"He was a bit mad anyway. But I had to do something, and I was sure that Tom would get there before me. I just need to be more careful in the future."

"Yes, dear," said Betty. "Especially in your condition."

"Betty, I've just run a mini marathon in record time. I'm in very good condition."

"Not that sort, dear. You know, for a psychic, you can't see what's literally under your very nose."

"What are you talking about?" said Terry, who was equally puzzled.

"You're a man, so you're forgiven for being slow," said Abigail.

"What?!" said Hayley.

"Well, I was a nurse."

"And I'm a grandmother."

"And I'm just nosy," said Abigail.

"WHAT?"

"You're going to have a baby!" they all said together.

"No. Really? No."

"Yes," said Suzie. "Even I knew."

"What makes you think so?"

Lillian counted on her fingers. "One—you're always tired, and not just from the run. Two—you seemed to be the only one that felt sick after the burgers that day. Three—you've put on a bit of weight, if you don't mind me saying."

"Yes, but if you exercise, they say your fat turns to muscles."

"In that case, you've got a very muscly stomach."

"Four—you have been a bit tetchy lately, and a bit emotional. And you've been hallucinating. I couldn't see that man you reckoned was called Benjamin," said Abigail.

"He was there, I'm sure. But do you really think I am? Tom will be delighted. I thought it took months and months to happen."

"Not always, dear. My John was very fertive. He only had to look at me," Betty said seriously.

Suzie asked, "Do you think it will be a girl or a boy, Hayley?"

"Now that I do know. I see a boy. I have done for ages. I just got the timing wrong."

"I can't believe we are going to have a baby," said Abigail. "Terry, we're going to be an auntie and uncle."

"I was hoping you could both be godparents."

"Wonderful. Even better. Thank you so much. Suzie, you can be the big sister, and Lillian can be the fun aunt."

"And I'll be his nana."

Abigail added, "We won't let anything happen to him, Hayley. We'll watch him night and day. If he so much as moves at night, we'll come and wake you up."

"Please don't. But I know you'll all be there for him, and me."

"So will you call him Terry?" he said hopefully.

"Probably not, to be honest. We'd better let Tom have a say in that."

"Have you seen his future in a vision? Is he going to be a doctor, or a pilot?"

"The only thing I know is that he's going to have the gift. I wouldn't be surprised if it's more than mine."

"So he'll be able to see us," said Suzie excitedly.

"I reckon so. I don't think Tom will be too pleased, but he'll love him so much that he won't care. I suppose I'd better do a test."

"Ooh, do it now."

"Sorry, Abi, I think it's something I should do with Tom. Let's face it, the husband is usually the first to know."

"If you insist. But we're going to come and see you first thing in the morning to check on you. Don't forget you've been through a lot tonight. We very nearly lost you and our baby. That's why we were making a fuss after that man attacked you. We didn't want anything to happen to our baby."

"It makes me shudder when I think of it. But at least this has taken my mind off that man. Let me have a lie-in then, please. I know you lot, you'd be here at seven if I let you. I've got some emails to write and make some appointments for readings. Then I'll go to the chemist and get a pregnancy test!"

Tom wondered what was going on when he got home the following night. He expected to see Hayley on the sofa, or still in shock, but here she was sitting at the table with candles lit. She didn't even want to hear what had happened to Martin Smith after his arrest. That definitely wasn't like her.

"Hiya. What's going on here? Is there a power cut?" he joked. "It's not our anniversary, is it? If it is, I've forgotten, and you can't really blame me with all that's happened."

"No, it's not our anniversary. Although, that shows you don't know when it is. You're about two months out. You haven't forgotten anything, and I haven't smashed the car. I just wanted to give you a nice supper. Sit down, hun. I'll get the starter."

"Starter? I am being spoiled."

Hayley walked back in and put a plate with a cover on it in front of him.

"Wow, thank you. I am hungry. It's … Is that what I think it is? Oh my God, Hayley, are you sure?"

"Of course I am. Look, it's got two lines."

"That means nothing to me. And you're sure, you know, the other way?"

"I am, hun. I even know the sex. Do you want to know?"

"Yes. No. Maybe. No, actually, I don't. Am I the first one you've told?"

"Of course." Well, in theory, they had told her.

"Come here. Sit on my lap. Oh yes, you're definitely heavier," he laughed.

"Cheeky monkey. I'll be getting a lot bigger than this. I have a feeling that he's going to be tall like his dad. Oh, sorry."

"A boy. Wow. That's even more perfect. I can take him to football."

"You don't go to football."

"Well, I'll start. Do you feel okay? Should I be doing anything?"

"Apparently pregnant women aren't allowed to do the hoovering or housework anymore."

"Okay, I can do that."

"Bless you. It's okay; I can do everything I did before," Hayley assured him.

"Except finding murderers, of course."

"I promise to be a lot more careful after tonight, Tom. But let's not let that madman ruin this moment." Luna came down the stairs from his double bed upstairs and wondered what was going on. He couldn't believe she was sitting on his lap. That was his spot. Not wanting to miss out, he jumped on Hayley's lap and got tickles from both of them.

"Someone might be a bit jealous," said Tom. "He's got used to being the baby."

"We'll still make a fuss of you. You'll always be our firstborn, Lu. He'll love having another little one to play with." Luna wasn't sure what they were talking about, but something had changed. They better not be going away again, that was all.

"Will you go and see your parents, Hayley, or tell them over the phone?"

"I'll go and visit when I get the chance. But I'll probably tell Mum on the phone tomorrow. I can't wait. She'll be over the moon."

Tom squeezed her. "You've made me so happy, babe. Mum and Dad are always mentioning it. And they live close, so we'll always have a babysitter."

"And we'll have Abigail and the gang. They'll probably never leave him alone."

"Oh God, I'd forgotten about them."

"Don't forget when Suzie's brother was bullied, she made sure that never happened again, hun. And look what Suzie did tonight. Our child will have all the spiritual protection it needs."

"Like a guardian angel, I suppose. Or a bodyguard. As long

as they're not here more than usual. They're not here now, are they?"

"No, of course not. What do you think your mum will say?"

"She'll be buying all the booties and little hats."

"I was going to knit them."

"Okay, I'll tell her to get plenty then."

"I'll have you know, I'm sure I'll be really good at it. I had a look online, and it looks easy."

"If you say so. Mum's already tried to name the baby. Louise if it's a girl, after her mum. And if it's a boy, she'd like to name it after her grandad. She was very close to him because her dad died when she was young. Even if we have it for a middle name."

"It's not one of those really old-fashioned ones like Humphrey, is it?"

"Actually, I rather like it, Hayley. It's Benjamin."

Hayley then understood her silent vision. "In that case, tell her I love the name. And I think her grandad will be very happy about it. In fact, I can honestly say, I think he'll be speechless!"

Chapter 33

"Interview commencing 10.05 a.m. Martin Arnold Smith is in the room with myself, DCI Johnson, and Sergeant Mills. You've been read your rights and refused a lawyer, is that right?"

"That is correct." Smith looked straight ahead—not at the two policemen, but above their heads.

"You have been arrested for the attempted murder of Mrs Hayley Bennett in the village of Chortle." Johnson put his hand over his mouth and said to his colleague, "I've felt like it myself."

"That is correct."

"Well, this is the easiest interview we've had to do yet, isn't it, Mills? Look, I know Mrs Bennett can be a busybody, but why did you see fit to bash her head in with a hammer?"

"It was nothing personal. She just happened to be there. I had already decided I would hit the first person that I saw that night."

"And why was that, if you don't mind telling us for the tape?"

"Not at all. It was the village I was punishing. As it says in the Good Book, an eye for an eye."

"What good book would that be? You see, I don't read any books, good or bad."

"The Holy Bible, of course."

"Ah, I don't hold with that either. I'm what's called an atheist. Or is it agnostic? Maybe both."

"Then I feel sorry for you. My mother brought me up to read it every night. And I would be punished if I strayed from His teaching."

"That explains a lot. Bit of a nutter herself, was she?"

"Don't you dare talk about Mother like that. She was a saint." Then Martin Smith smiled sweetly. "But 'judge not, condemn not, forgive and you will be forgiven'. I will add you to my prayer list."

"I think you'd be better praying for yourself, sir. I've got your file here; it seems that you were arrested once before."

"But no charges were brought. And I was young, before I became a minister of the Lord."

"Let's see, you were accused of what we now call stalking. You were harassing a lady who didn't feel the same way as you. Back then, you sent her multiple flowers with notes. For the tape, I'm showing Mr Smith one of the cards, on which it says, 'Suffer in hell, Jezebel'. Very poetic, I'm sure. You were cautioned, but not charged."

"That is correct."

"So that brings us to the present attack. Did Hayley Bennett spurn your advances like this poor lady?"

"Don't be ridiculous. I have no interest in women. I serve only God. Not some floozie. And thinking about it, she was stalking me. I swear she's the lady that grabbed me the other day when I was going back to my flat."

"I must tell you that Hayley Bennett is married to a policeman, so don't give us any of that rubbish. I'm sure she wouldn't be interested in a slovenly scruff like you. So we must presume that it's the same motives as the others."

"What others? I tell you that I have no interest in the opposite sex."

"The other murders, Mr Smith."

The man rubbed his hand through his long, stringy hair and swallowed hard. For the first time, he looked Johnson in the eye. "As God is my witness, I have no idea what you are talking about."

"Unfortunately, He's not going to be much of a witness, is He? We're obviously a lot better at our jobs than you were at yours, Reverend. They got rid of you at Great Heron, didn't they? It says here you were the vicar there."

Martin's eyes widened. "I was, for over twenty years, and I was good at my job. Ask anyone. The whole congregation loved me."

"But when Bishop Carlysle refused to change his mind, you decided to make them pay."

"I wasn't the only one that lost their job. Talk to Julian Drake."

"We have. He hasn't turned into a homicidal maniac. Just a teacher of Religious Studies at a secondary school. But you started killing one person in every church in your parish every year. And as good policemen, we worked out that you killed three people on the anniversary of the sacking. This time of year, in fact."

"How can you know that? It's complete rubbish. I'm a religious man. I live by the Bible."

"Oh yes, because there aren't any murders or revenge killings in that, are there? Or do you just cherry-pick the bits that suit you?"

"What about an eye for an eye?"

"Or turn the other cheek. Or Thou shalt not kill. Even I know that one. Look, we can argue about it all day, but the truth of it is, I'm going to throw the proverbial book at you. And no, I don't mean the Bible. Luckily for us, you kindly left your DNA on the quotes at the murder scenes, so now we can check it against yours. Our crime scene investigators are going through your flat now. I think you're stupid. I bet we're going to find all the evidence we need. You've got to have smarts to get away with murder. There's going to be traces of blood on your clothes. And I bet Sergeant Mills here, a pint of best that you didn't have the brains to get rid of the knife that you used on George Buttler. I bet you washed it and put it back in the drawer. I bet it's…"

"I didn't; I threw it down a drain," Smith shouted, and then his body crumpled. Mother was going to be angry.

Sergeant Mills spoke for the first time. "Martin Arnold Smith, you are charged with the murders of Beryl Carstairs, Cindy Doyle, George Buttler, and the attempted murder of Hayley Bennett."

Chapter 34

ONCE AGAIN, HAYLEY WAS IN THE GROUNDS OF THE Courtridge Hotel. This time she was joined by Tom and the owners of the hotel, Maria and Anita Dubois. The autumn leaves had long since left the branches, and the ground was hard and cold. The bench that once Hayley and Bones had sat on was now nearer to Deadman's Pond, and crime scene tape was blowing in the breeze on the exact spot where it had once been.

Two weeks earlier, Bob and his groundsmen at the hotel had been shocked to find a skull in the exact spot that the boss had said she wanted a summerhouse. After that, the police had taken over the scene. They had found a whole skeleton and a faded red-handled cricket bat, on which was a good set of fingerprints. Bob was only just beginning to get over the shock and told the lads at the pub that it was the body of a young teenager who went missing years ago. Killed by a drug dealer, he had heard. But after an autopsy, he'd been laid to rest. Apparently, he told them, his mum had taken his ashes down to Cornwall, where she lived with her other son. Bob said he was a musician of some sort. They went back to their game of darts, and Elliot Thornton soon became last week's news.

The Deadly Fun Run

"So, Mrs Dubois, Hayley tells me you're going to do ghost walks and paranormal weekends," said Tom.

"We are, and murder mystery evenings. Thankfully, your wife says she'll help out. She seems to know where all the ghosts are. It's just a shame that we missed Halloween."

"I don't think it makes much difference to Hayley. She seems to be haunted all year round. Especially by someone called Abigail."

"Funnily enough, she's not here today. Only because she's going somewhere herself. But I'm so looking forward to the ghost tours. Sir Whittlebury gave me the perfect route—past Hangman's Hill and down Peasants' Path. And you need to look up what happened to the witches that were drowned right over there. I talked to Elliot's mother, and she had no problem with the walk ending here. She thinks it's great that his name will be kept alive, as long as we don't mention the one who killed him by name. He doesn't deserve to be remembered for anything. And as she says, if it wasn't for the paranormal, we would never have known what happened to him. He'd just be another missing son and suspected murderer."

"We'll do it respectfully for all the dead," said Anita.

"How will it work? Have you got someone in mind to lead them round?"

Maria said, "We don't know whether to get an actor or get a local ghost hunter to say what he knows. I think we'll probably do that, and then they can have a percentage of any tickets sold. Depending on the appeal, we'll probably do that fortnightly. Every few months we may do a murder mystery experience, and then hold a paranormal event one weekend a month. We're hoping you could do something for that. For a fee, of course."

"I'd be delighted to. You'd be surprised how much I do for free. I do have one favour I need to ask you. Suzie is a young spirit friend of mine, and she'll be so great for here, as she's actually a poltergeist. But they call her a Mover. Can you imagine what they'll think when something goes flying across the room? You'd better put on the advert, 'not for the faint-hearted'. It seems to be just children who have these powers. But her mother is a social worker, and I happen to know that she could really do with one of your pampering spa weekends. She's had a hard time since her little girl died."

"It would be our pleasure. We do gift vouchers, so come back to the office. She can have the luxury five-star one. It's a two-night stay for her and a friend, with all the meals and treatments included. I'm sure we can throw in some extras as well."

"I can't wait to tell Suzie. Thank you so much. And I promise I'll do some star charts and tarot cards. Or even one-on-one readings. You could charge more for those."

"That would be amazing, Hayley."

"You could charge double to let them stay overnight in a haunted room."

"Have we got any?"

"You will have," she laughed. "Tell them room thirty-four is haunted, and you can charge what you like. Then in the daytime, you can do fortune telling, get some other mediums in, and sell some crystals and dreamcatchers even. You'll make a fortune—excuse the pun."

"We're going to get some leaflets made. It's so exciting. We're just glad there's nothing where we live. We'd never sleep."

Tom was just going to tell them that that was where Sir Timothy walked, until Hayley elbowed him in the ribs.

"But we've heard that you two have some exciting news of your own. It was Lady Caroline who told us. I hope you don't mind."

Hayley took Tom's hand. "Let's face it, I'll be showing soon anyway. Yes, we're having our own little Benjamin. Well, Benjie."

"I love that name. When is the baby due, Hayley?"

"In the spring. New season, new life."

"We can't wait to have our own little Dubois," said Maria. "My dad was over from the States and made it clear that he wanted a grandchild before he got too old."

"My mum was the same," said Tom. "It was her that got us thinking about it. She gave me a knitted orange and white bunny that she'd kept from when I was a child to give us a hint. Do you remember, Hayl?"

"Remember? It still gives me nightmares. Mind you, it's better than I could make. I've tried my hand at knitting a pair of booties, and as long as Benjie has one foot bigger than the other, they'll be fine."

"It's a dying art. But I did hear it's starting to get more popular," said Maria.

"Really? Or perhaps I should try crochet."

"Or just buy them," said Tom.

"Good idea. Maybe I'll make a blue shawl. Surely that's easy. It's only a square."

"I'm surprised you know it's a boy already. I thought they couldn't tell till so many months."

"Ah, well, it's not official, as through a doctor. But I have it on very good authority that it will be a gorgeous little boy," said Tom.

"Who from?" asked Maria.

"My gorgeous wife," Tom said proudly.

Chapter 35

OVER IN CHORTLE A YOUNG GIRL WAS STANDING BY A window, waiting to see a car pull into the lane. Anya was waiting for her father to come home for the first time in nearly two years. That sounded good; her daddy coming home. Her world had been turned upside down since two policemen had knocked at their door at five o'clock one morning. But now it was over.

She didn't understand all the legal terms that she'd heard on the news—miscarriage of justice or wrongly convicted. She just knew that Daddy was coming home this morning.

Some of the press were there, but most had promised to give them their privacy as long as they got interviews in the near future. There were a few false alarms, like when the postman went past, and again when the taxi dropped off Mrs Harris after her hospital appointment. But when Anya and her mother thought they couldn't stand it any more, a blue car pulled up outside.

Anya smiled when she saw that nice policeman, Sergeant Mills, get out of the driver's seat and wait for her dad to get out. Anya's smile faded when she saw him. He looked so old and grey and thin. But she wouldn't show it, so she ran to the front door. Anne stood next to her and didn't even notice the cameras flashing as her husband walked quickly towards them. Grant Finn went in and shut the door on the rest of the world.

"My girls. I've missed you so much." Anya had been up to his waist last time he had been able to hug her, and now she reached his chest. Another reminder of how much of her life he had missed. "And look at my beautiful little girl looking all grown up."

"Oh, Grant, we've missed you so much."

"I don't know how you did this, Anne, but I'm so glad you did."

"I'm so happy. Come and sit down. I'm not sure either. I hired this strange woman, Hayley Moon. Even that was strange; I had a card come through the door and something told me I had to ask for her help. She came to see me, and before I knew it, they found the man that really killed that poor girl. But I never did pay her, and she didn't want any publicity. Or for it to get out that she had anything to do with it. She was even there when they caught him. Honestly, she was like a guardian angel or something."

"We need to write a letter of thanks. And how's my lovely little Anya getting on? I hear you're at big school now. Do you miss St Nicholas School for Girls?"

"No, I don't, Daddy. I've got a new best friend, called Camille. You'll like her. She doesn't live far and she's been so nice since she found out about you. I think I'd much rather stay where I am."

"Probably just as well. It's going to be a while till I get another job and get on my feet."

Anne said, "I was told you'll be getting compensation, Grant."

"I know, but that could take months. I'm just happy to be home." He looked around for the first time. "It's a bit different to Gladstone Forge, isn't it? I'm so sorry you lost the house, Anne."

"I didn't care so much about that as losing you," replied his wife.

"I know, darling. It'll do for now. It's a lot better than..." Grant's head started to shake.

"Oh, don't, Daddy. Don't be upset. You're home now. Let me make you a cup of tea."

"You can make a cup of tea? When did that happen? You weren't allowed to touch the kettle last I knew."

"Oh, Daddy. I'm eleven and a half now."

"Are you sure?" he joked. "It'll take a lot of getting used to. I've got a lot to catch up on. I'd love a cup of tea, darling. And I promise I'll never leave you again."

Lillian, Suzie and Betty had been watching, and now went on their way back to Becklesfield. They would never get a thank you, but the sight of the reunion was gratitude enough.

Betty said, "Will he ever get over it, do you think? He was putting on a brave face, but he was definitely struggling."

"It'll take a while for all of them. Especially Anya. But children are remarkably resilient."

"I'm glad she's not going back to her private school. I was so happy she was best friends with my Camille."

"She'll stay there, I think. I reckon they'll move to a better house, but it will be in this area. I know he'll get compensation for being in prison for a crime he didn't commit, but that will take a while. So I wouldn't worry, Suzie."

Betty put her arms through both her friends, "I think we can be very proud of ourselves, you know. We released one man from prison, and another one from his grave. The Deadly Detective Agency is the best."

"It is," said Suzie. "And we mustn't forget Celia at the newspaper. I wonder what the next case will be."

Lillian said, "We did really well, but to be honest, I could do without a murder for a while. Let's head for Ridgeway Wood and forget about crime. I wonder how Terry and Abigail are getting on. It's a lovely day for a trip to the seaside."

Terry and Abigail were still walking to the train station at Halton Thorpe. Terry had spent the last ten minutes giving Abigail a lecture on how all the small stations were shut in the sixties, by someone called Beeching. Abigail was almost pleased when she noticed a lady waving. She turned around to see who she was talking to, but there was no one behind her.

The middle-aged woman, dressed in a blue dress and cardigan, crossed the road and came right up to them. "Abigail, how very serendipitous to see you. Do you remember me, Carol Newsome?"

"Um, I think so," she said, frowning.

"My husband and I are going on a cruise to South America shortly. He's had an enormous bonus from work. He didn't give me the details. Just told me to go and get a whole new wardrobe. So I've got loads that need altering. Evening gowns, jackets, you name it. Do you think you could fit me in? I do hope you're not too busy. It's funny, I'm sure someone said you weren't doing it anymore."

Abigail looked at Terry for help. "Actually, I'm not."

"Oh no, you were so good at it. And reasonable. I've been going to that shop in Gorebridge and they charge a fortune. Why did you stop?"

"I was murdered," said Abigail bluntly.

Terry took over. "I think we need to have a talk, Mrs Newsome. Come and sit down with me. I'm sorry, Abi, this won't take long. Ten minutes, twenty tops."

"Okay then. But I bet this never happened in that romantic film that Hayley was telling me about. The one set on a train—Close Encounter."

"It's Brief."

"You'd better bloody be. I'm not waiting around all day."

Terry gave her a kiss and laughed. "I do love you, you daft sausage."

Abigail wondered what she had said that was so funny. But he said he loved her; that was the most important thing. And they could always get the next train. She thought how kind and patient Terry was to the poor lady when he started telling her that unfortunately she had passed, as he led her to a wall to sit on.

It was then that Abigail noticed the round mark on the back of her white cardigan, and the red stain that ran from it. She had never seen one before, but she had watched enough detective shows to know that it was a bullet hole.

Carol Newsome was about to find out that not only was she dead, she wouldn't be going on a cruise to South America. And somehow, Abigail had to break the news to Terry that the train would be leaving without them. They better go and find Hayley and the others—The Deadly Detective Agency had another murder to solve.

THE END

Acknowledgments

A special thank you to Miika Hannila at Next Chapter Publishing.
And to Petteri Hannila for the excellent layout.
Also, many thanks to Lordan June Pinote,
who has done another excellent cover.

About the Author

Ann Parker was born in Hertfordshire, England and still lives there with her husband, Terry, and her black and white cat, Jazz.

She is the author of the Abigail Summers Cozy Mysteries—The Deadly Detective Agency, The Deadly Pub Quiz, The Deadly Regatta and The Deadly Fun Run.

Her children's short stories are available in the book entitled *Magic & Memories*.

Ann has had poems published on Spillwords and in best-selling anthologies, *Hidden in Childhood* and *Petals of Haiku*, as well as various magazines.

When she is not writing, she loves to spend time with her family or reading a good whodunit.

To learn more about Ann Parker and discover more Next Chapter authors, visit our website at www.nextchapter.pub.

Printed in Dunstable, United Kingdom